PONY CLU

© 1979 Norman Thelwell
N. thelwell.
This book belongs to
F. PIPER

Also in Armada

Plenty of Ponies
Prince Among Ponies
Pony Club Camp
Show Jumping Secret
One Day Event
Race Horse Holiday
The Trick Jumpers

PONY CLUB TEAM

JOSEPHINE PULLEIN-THOMPSON

First published in the U.K. in 1972 by
William Collins Sons & Co. Ltd., Glasgow.
First published in this edition in Armada in 1973 by
Fontana Paperbacks, 14 St. James's Place,
London SW1A 1PS.

This impression 1980.

Printed in Great Britain by
Love & Malcomson Ltd., Brighton Road,
Redhill, Surrey.

CHAPTER ONE

THE rally was over. The Pony Club members rode down the two long, gravelled drives away from Folly Court. The five red-headed Radcliffes, the three Minton boys—two on ponies and one riding a bicycle—and June Cresswell were the only members to take the drive which led to the Hogshill road. The Radcliffes, all talking at the tops of their voices, were in front.

"I thought it was a good rally," said James, the youngest Radcliffe present.

"Well, you haven't been to as many as we have," said Evelyn, one of the fourteen-year-old twins. "When you have you won't be so keen on them; all this schooling gets jolly boring, I can tell you."

"I hate it," said Margaret, "and so does Pixie. I do think Major Holbrooke *might* let us have some races for a change."

"Oh, you're never satisfied," said Hilary, the other twin. "Surely we did enough jumping to-day?"

"It wasn't bad," answered Margaret. "But he *never* lets us have a jumping competition; you just go on and on going over the same potty little jumps."

"If you jumped them decently he might let you try something higher," Roger, the eldest of the Radcliffes, told her.

"Well, at least I don't fall off all the time like the Mintons," answered Margaret.

"You would if you had to ride Fireworks or Mousie," said Hilary.

"And it's better to fall off than to look like a windmill," added Roger.

"All the same, I agree with Marga," said Evelyn. "It's time Georgie Holbrooke thought of something besides this eternal schooling—it's all right for the little ones, but the rest of us know it by heart."

"I disgraced myself to-day," said Christopher Minton to his two brothers, David and Martin. "Three times is a record for one rally, I should think. You are an old devil," he added, patting Fireworks, a black gelding of about fourteen hands.

"Mousie was good for her," said David, "and Major Holbrooke said that she had improved."

"A lot of people fell off, didn't they?" said Christopher. "Noel Kettering and Pat French and me and Simon and that new girl on the big brown."

"And Virginia Freeman," said David.

"Do get that bicycle out of the way," interrupted a peevish voice from behind them. "I know Golden Glory's going to tread on it if you keep twisting about in front of her and I don't want her blemished."

"Look out David; you'd better let June come past," said Christopher to his younger brother. "Your horse walks too fast for us," he said politely.

"Of course she does," answered June. "Any horse can walk faster than a pony and one of the judges at the Barsetshire Show said that Glory had an exceptionally long stride, even for a thoroughbred."

"That girl gets me down," remarked Christopher when June was out of hearing.

Four of the pupils from the Basset Riding School led the way down the drive to the Brampton-Lower Basset road. They were clattering along at a fast trot, which would have horrified Mrs. Maxton—the owner of the school—had she seen them, and which shocked Noel Kettering, John Manners and Susan Barington-Brown, who followed some distance behind.

"The Major wasn't in a very good temper to-day, was he?" said Susan.

"No, filthy," agreed John. "Everyone was being ticked off right and left."

"I'm not surprised considering the crowd we had," said Noel. "It must be awfully difficult when they range from Martin Minton and James Radcliffe to Anthony Rate and that new girl, who are practically grown up. It's not like it was last summer when *none* of us knew anything, we're all at different stages."

"It's quite true," said John, "and it would be much more fun without all these little ones; like it was in the days of the horse-breakers." Noel thought of the summer holidays the year before when she and John and Susan had been breaking in three of Major Holbrooke's cousin's New Forest ponies. She patted her grey pony, Sonnet, which had been her prize as the best horse-breaker. "That was fun," said said, "but of course there were only six of us."

"I wish we could do something like that again," said John.

"*I* wish we could have a Pony Club camp," said Susan, "other branches do."

"The Radcliffes asked the Major," said John, pulling up Dick Turpin, his roan cob, for now they had reached the road, "and he said that they could have as many camps as they liked if they found someone to organise them."

"I do wish there *was* someone nice who would run a camp," said Susan. "I should love to sleep out and I'm never allowed to at home."

"Why on earth not?" asked John.

"Oh, Mummy's fussy," answered Susan.

"Well, good-bye," said John. "See you at test day on

Tuesday. I'm sure I shan't pass 'B' but my father's promised me a pound if I do, so I'm going to make superhuman efforts."

"Of course you'll pass," said Susan, and Noel asked, "Why did you have to remind me? Now I've got the needle."

"Oh, Noel, you can't have," said Susan as they turned towards Brampton.

"You always say that," said Noel, "but I have got it, honestly. Beauty jumped jolly well to-day," she went on, looking at Susan's brown pony. "I wish that Sonnet was better, but I do think she's improving. It takes such ages to school a horse." She sighed, "I don't think she'll be ready for the gymkhana."

"That's ages away," said Susan.

"But I've got to go away on this beastly expedition of Daddy's," said Noel. "Waste a whole fortnight while he lectures on Egyptian relics or something. I'm fed up, I can tell you."

"Oh, dear," said Susan, "and Daddy says I'm too big for Beauty. It's really Mummy's fault; she's getting a bit horsy at last and she keeps telling Daddy that I look a sight on Beauty. But I'm not going to sell her, I've made that quite clear; I'm going to go on riding her a bit and lend her to friends occasionally and next year I might breed from her."

"That's a good idea," said Noel.

"Are you coming over to school to-morrow?" asked Susan, when she reached the gate of her house.

"No, I don't think so," answered Noel. "Sonnet had better have a rest. She's had a fairly strenuous time to-day and she's only a five-year-old and not at all fit."

"Well, I'll come over to Russet Cottage then," said Susan. "I want you to ask me some questions; I'm sure I don't know enough Stable Management for 'B' test."

"O.K.," said Noel.

Major and Mrs. Holbrooke were having tea in the garden at Folly Court. The Major swallowed his fifth egg sandwich and handed his empty cup to his wife for some more tea. "This weather's far too hot for Pony Club rallies," he said. "Those children have nearly killed me."

"You had a lot to-day, didn't you?" asked Mrs. Holbrooke. "I only watched from the windows—I steered clear of the paddock because I felt in no mood for mothers—but there seemed to be dozens of children."

"Yes, dozens," agreed the Major, "and all equally hopeless."

"Oh, George, how can you?" said his wife. "Your cousin Harry's always telling you . . ."

"Harry's a fool," interrupted Major Holbrooke. "Just because the standard of riding is higher here than in some Pony Clubs, he thinks we should all pat ourselves on the back and relax. What these children don't realise," he went on, "is that anyone, who is properly taught, can reach the stage which they have, but it is only by their own effort and energy that they will go beyond it."

"But you can't expect everyone to take riding as seriously as you do," said Mrs. Holbrooke. "After all, there are tennis and swimming, the theatre and the cinema and a hundred other amusements to fill the time left by school and homework."

"Well, there's a certain responsibility in having a horse or pony," said the Major. "You can't treat it like a tennis racket and if they're going to ride they must leave out a few of the other amusements and take it seriously."

"I don't see how you're going to persuade them to do that," said Mrs. Holbrooke. The Major helped himself to a slice of chocolate cake.

"If I could get hold of a few of the very keen ones," he said thoughtfully, "and give them some really concentrated instruction for about a week or ten days, I believe that I could show them what real riding is like and then, afterwards, they would always have something at which to aim."

"Well, if it's only a week or ten days, why don't you have them?" asked Mrs. Holbrooke.

"Have them?" said the Major. "But my dear Carol, the keen members are scattered all over Barsetshire and I can't teach dressage to children mounted on unfit ponies, which have already hacked seven or eight miles."

"Can't we have the ponies to stay?" suggested Mrs. Holbrooke. "And the children, too, for that matter. It would be rather fun; this place has been much too quiet lately."

"There certainly wouldn't be any quiet if we had half the Pony Club staying here," said the Major, "and I don't suppose much of the place would be left standing either."

"They'd be nice friends for Henry," said Mrs. Holbrooke. "I suppose that you've forgotten that your nephew is coming to stay for three weeks?"

"I had forgotten," said the Major. "I suppose I shall have to find something for him to ride. Well, I'll think over this mad scheme of yours and I might sound the members at the test day next week."

The industry among the members of the West Barsetshire Pony Club was quite exceptional during the weekend before test day. Every one seemed to be borrowing books on stable management from everyone else and then persuading their brothers, sisters, friends or parents to ask them the points of the horse or questions about splints and spavins.

"A horse's temperature in health is between 99 degrees and 101 degrees," muttered Noel as she collected an apple and a halter with which to catch Sonnet. "Young horses and thoroughbreds have higher temperatures than ordinary horses. There are two kinds of colic; spasmodic and flatulent," she murmured as she climbed the gate into Farmer Trent's forty-acre meadow where Sonnet was turned out. I'm sure I shall fail, she thought, as she walked towards the four chestnut trees, under which Sonnet always sheltered on hot days.

Noel's heart filled, as always, with love and pride when her little grey mare whinnied and appeared from the shadow of the trees. Sonnet might not be a show pony but with her finely-made head, which had a faintly Arabian look about it, her kind eye, dappled coat and darker mane and tail, she was everything that Noel desired. One day she would be a good jumper and really well-schooled, but at the moment life was rather disheartening; it seemed that when at last the term with its prep and netball matches was over, one's parents merely dragged one away from one's pony to go on a lecturing tour. Noel rode Sonnet back across the field and put her into the loose-box, which Professor Kettering had bought for her when he had been paid the royalties on his book about Egypt. Then, fetching *The Complete Horsemaster,* Noel settled down under an apple tree in the garden. "Laminitis or fever of the feet is an inflamed condition of the fleshy leaves beneath the wall of the hoof and covering the coffin bone," she read.

Down at Lower Basset Farm, John Manners shut his book with an angry bang. He was fed up with buffers and rasps and pritchels; his head felt stuffy and his eyes ached; he was sure that he knew less about shoeing than when he had begun. He would take Turpin for a ride, a ride with a gallop so that he could forget all about test day. After all it would be bad enough when he failed, without ruining his life beforehand. For once Turpin was in a field close to the farm so it didn't take long to bring him into the stable.

No risen clenches, thought John, looking at his shoes, and I see Hodges shod you with rolled toes behind.

In the playroom at Fenchurch House, David was testing Christopher. "Another name for the second thigh?" he asked.

"Oh gosh," said Christopher, who was sitting on the big scrubbed deal table, "don't say I've forgotten that *again.* You, know, I have."

"Gaskin, you fathead," said David, and Martin who was crawling about on the floor setting out their jointly owned railway said, "You'll never pass 'B'."

"No, I haven't the ghost of a chance," agreed Christopher, "but I expect I shall get 'C', everyone says that it's easy." "Ssh," said David, "I'm going to ask you another; what is a stargazer?"

"Oh, I know *that,*" said Christopher. "It's a horse which sticks its head in the air and looks at the sky. They're awfully difficult to stop; they bang you on the nose and you have to ride them in martingales."

"Come on," said Martin. "Surely that's enough; the trains are all ready and the eleven-two is getting up steam."

"One more question," said David, turning over several pages at once. "How many pounds of oats does a fourteen-hand pony, doing regular work, need a day?"

"A bucketful," said Christopher, "but I haven't an idea how many pounds that would be."

"Well, guess," said David.

"Hurry up," added Martin.

"Three pounds," guessed Christopher.

"No," said David, "this book says, 'a fourteen-hand pony which is being worked regularly may have from five to eight pounds of oats daily.' Still I suppose three is better than nothing."

"I wonder how many oats Fireworks and Mousie have?" said Christopher. "Not nearly as much as that I'm sure."

"Do stop bothering about that stupid test, Mummy," said June Cresswell. "I'm sure that *I* know enough for it since Major Holbrooke said that Noel and Susan and John were good enough to try."

"Now, June dear, do listen a moment to what I have to say," said Mrs. Cresswell, a sharp-featured woman with severely waved iron-grey hair. "I'm quite satisfied that your riding is well above the standard required; you know more about hunting than most of the Associates, whatever airs they may put on, but it's your stable management, my pet, that worries me, for Wilson does the greater part of your stable work, but some of those children do every bit themselves and that gives them an advantage."

"Oh, Mummy, how can you be so silly?" asked June. "What they do isn't stable management. They just drag their common muddy animals in and out of the field, brush them with a dandy brush and throw them a bit of hay in the winter. They don't know anything about looking after a pony *properly*; they've hardly ever seen rugs and bandages."

"Well, perhaps you're right, my dear," said Mrs. Cresswell, "but you can't trust them; you know how they tried to do you down at the gymkhana last year; I really think that you should read the chapter on first aid in the veterinary book and ask Hodges to give you a few tips on shoeing."

"Hodges doesn't know anything," replied June. "He said that Glory had thin soles and flat feet."

"I don't think our theory's too bad," said Roger Radcliffe, sitting on the edge of the stable water butt, "but has anyone an idea how to put on leg bandages?"

"Not a clue," replied Evelyn, who was lying on a patch of grass nearby. "Anyway I think it's a silly thing to ask Pony Club members to do, because ponies never need their legs bandaged—it's only thoroughbred weeds with no bone."

"Oh, Evelyn," said Hilary, "don't you remember the rally at the end of the Christmas holidays after Roger had gone back to school? Blake—you know, the Major's stud groom—showed us how to put them on and explained their different uses."

"I remember the rally vaguely," said Evelyn, rolling over on her back, "it was frightfully dull."

"Well, there were exercise bandages," said Hilary. "Those were for support, rather the same idea as wearing a strap round one's wrist for tennis. One put them on as tightly as possible over cotton wool. They only covered the cannon bone, but the stable bandages—which were made of a sort of woolly flannel, as far as I remember—were put on very loosely and they began right up by the knee or hock and went right over the fetlock and back up the leg again. There's probably lots more that I've forgotten," she went on, "so we'd better look it up somewhere."

"I suppose that we could practise both kinds with tail bandages," said Roger, "unless Doc's got a flannel bandage in the surgery that would do."

Dick Hayward, brown-haired and brown-eyed and small for his age, which was sixteen, wasn't bothering about "B" test because he had passed it the summer holidays before last, when Miss Mitchell had been running the pony club; but, he decided, he might as well ride over to Folly Court on Tuesday. Pony Club rallies were always good value and he had missed the last one because it had been his coaching day. If he ever finished being crammed for "O" levels, thought Dick, he would re-read all his horsy books and have a shot at "A" test. As he crossed the field he decided that now he would put Crispin in the stable, away from the flies, and after tea, when it would be cooler, he would go for his favourite ride; along the Roman road, down Stark Dyke and home by the Hogshill bridle path.

"It's ridiculous," said Brigadier Hemlock-Jones angrily. "I don't know what Holbrooke's thinking of. I don't pay a man so that you shall spend your time looking after those horses, bandaging and tack cleaning and the whole business. How's White to occupy himself while you're doing all the work, may I ask?"

"But, Daddy darling," said Merry in her most soothing voice, "it isn't Major Holbrooke, it's the Pony Club, which sets the tests, and only the weeniest bit of it's on stable management; the rest's riding and how to behave in the hunting field."

"Well, they ought to fail the lot on their hunting manners," said the Brigadier firmly. "I've never seen such a lot of wretched little thrusters, never in my life; can't move for 'em."

"Oh, Daddy, you know you said that John Manners opened three gates for you when they met at Sledgers last season."

"And so he ought, so he ought," answered the Brigadier, slightly squashed.

"Well, darling, if I ever have a groom of my own I shan't be able to tell him where he's wrong if I don't know how things should be done."

"Always employ a first-class man and trust him implicitly," answered the Brigadier and then he added, "Well, run along and play at stable boy, if you must; I've got some important letters to write."

"Thank you, Daddy," said Merry, as she left the room. She changed her shoes for jodhpur boots and put on her perfectly tailored second best riding coat and then she hurried out to the stables.

"Hullo, darlings," she said to Quaver, her brown half-bred gelding and Crotchet, her chestnut three-quarter-bred mare. "Good morning, White," she said to her father's groom. "I want you to teach me how to rug up, bandage and clean tack; I'm going to take the pony club 'B' test next week."

"Pass?" said Mr. Barington-Brown to Susan. "Not likely. You've got a head like a sieve, you have, in one ear—out the other; you'll be bottom, that's where you'll be."

"Oh, Daddy, how can you?" said Susan. "I've got the needle badly enough now, without you making me worse. Anyway, I don't think that I shall quite be bottom because Christopher Minton's going in for it and he hasn't even taken 'C' yet."

"Well, I tell you what," said Mr. Barington-Brown, "if you pass I'll get you a couple of posh rugs with your initials in the corner—like the Major has. One for Beauty and one for this new pony."

"Oh goody," said Susan and then she added, "Oh dear, but I'm sure that I shan't pass."

CHAPTER TWO

THE ordeal was over; everyone had been examined. The examiners, Mrs. Hornsey, a hard woman to hounds, Captain Barton, an equitation expert, and Colonel Shellbourne, Major Holbrooke's cousin, Harry, had pocketed their notebooks, filled with fateful marks and were eating a delicious lunch in the long, white, Georgian dining-room of Folly Court.

The ponies had been watered and, tied to the iron railings, were eating their feeds; the Pony Club members sat or sprawled in the shade of an oak and discussed the examiners, the questions and who was likely to have passed.

"They weren't too bad," said John Manners, with his mouth full of cheese sandwich. "At least, they weren't as bad as I expected, but after all the trouble I took to learn about shoeing all they asked was how to tell when a pony needed new shoes; that was one of the questions when I took 'C'. I expected to be asked something about feather-edge shoes or pritchels or rolled toes."

"Thank goodness we weren't. I made some frightful bloomers as it was," said Christopher Minton gaily. "Honestly, I was a complete idiot. I said that a fourteen-hand pony needed eight pounds of *food* a day; I muddled it up with how many oats he was to have."

"I forgot where the gaskin was, but of course I've remembered now," said Susan. "That's just like me, and my stable bandages were terribly lumpy."

"The cotton wool kept slipping from under my exercise ones," said Noel. "I'm sure I haven't passed."

"Nor have I," said a chorus of voices.

"I was hopeless at adjusting the double bridle," said Roger Radcliffe, "but I did remember the difference between plints and spavins."

"So I should hope," said Evelyn.

"The riding part looked fairly easy," said Dick, who had been in charge of the jump all morning.

"It wasn't bad," said Susan, "but I expect I cantered on the wrong leg and didn't notice!"

"I'm sure that we can't *all* have failed," said June Cresswell.

"No, of course we can't," agreed Evelyn.

"I don't know," said Noel thoughtfully, "they asked such easy questions they probably expected very accurate answers."

"They didn't get much accuracy from me," said Christopher, "but they were decent—they gave me lots of hints."

"Here they are," said Susan.

"Prepare yourselves for the worst," said Roger.

"Cross your fingers," advised Christopher.

"They look in good tempers," remarked Noel

The children got to their feet, brushing the grass from their clothes and pushing their hair out of their eyes as the grown-ups approached, Colonel Shellbourne in the lead carrying the results. The Colonel told the members to gather round and then, having cleared his throat, he began, "I'm very glad to tell you, very glad indeed, that everyone has passed."

"Gosh," said the Pony Club members, looking at each other in surprise. Susan saw two ponies in elegant day rugs. John thought that with the pound his father had promised him he would be able to afford a new bridle for Turpin. June thought, there, I told Mummy I should pass;

she was a fool making me read that stupid book, even Christopher's passed. I expect I shall be top, but it depends whether they gave a lot of marks for riding.

Noel thought, hurray, and thank goodness that's over, and Christopher thought won't David and Martin be surprised? Roger thought, thank heavens, Evelyn thought I knew we would, and Hilary, I hope we've all got about the same marks.

"There were two or three rather near squeaks," Colonel Shellbourne went on. "I'll begin with the scraped throughs and work up the list. Virginia Freeman, Valentine Dale, Mary Crompton, Christopher Minton, Merry Hemlock-Jones. Then we have June Cresswell, Susan Barington-Brown, Evelyn Radcliffe, and then four of you who attained a really excellent standard; they were John Manners, Noel Kettering, Roger and Hilary Radcliffe. We were delighted with you four; you obviously had both your riding theory and your stable management at your finger-tips. I must add," the Colonel went on, "that I think it very creditable that you should all pass and, on behalf of my fellow examiners and myself, I congratulate you and, of course, Major Holbrooke. You must feel proud of them, George."

"Well, actually," said Major Holbrooke, looking rather ill-humoured, "I'm not at all proud of them. They're quite nice children and they ride quite nicely, but they're not horsemen yet. I've spent the last week trying to think of a way to improve your riding," he went on, turning and speaking to the members, "and now I have a plan. I want to find from six to twelve really keen people prepared to devote a fortnight of their holidays to improving themselves and their ponies. I propose to turn the ponies out here and my wife will put up one or two members if necessary. We will ride every morning, and sometimes in the afternoons—everyone will be expected to look after his own pony and clean his own tack. We shall do a certain amount of jumping and hacking, but most of our time will be devoted to dressage; that is, ordinary schooling done with greater precision and accuracy than is usual.

"Now I don't expect any answers to-day; you must ask your parents, but we shall start on Monday week."

"Think of it," said Evelyn, as she rode away from Folly Court, "a *fortnight's schooling*. Georgie Holbrooke must be stark staring mad if he thinks anyone will go."

"I don't know so much about that," said Roger. "It will improve Sky Pilot anyway."

"Get him behind the bit, you mean," said Evelyn.

"I should like to go," said Hilary, "but it's going to be a bit awkward over ponies. Rocket can't be expected to carry me every day for a fortnight." She patted her chestnut of thirteen hands as she spoke; he had been her pupil in the days of the horsebreakers and Dr. Radcliffe had bought him from Colonel Shellbourne.

"Well, I've already said that I don't want to go, so you can have Northwind if you want him," said Evelyn, "but don't blame me if he's completely ruined by this beastly dressage."

I do hope that Dad will let me, thought John, riding home along the shaded, winding road to Lower Basset, but we shall be harvesting, I suppose, and I know what that means. There's always tons to do. If I'm not actually carting I shall be doing all the jobs which no one else has got time to do. Anyway, Dad thinks dressage is silly. He'll say it's one of the Major's fads. Still, he ought to be in a good temper to-night, now that I've passed "B" test.

I shall go, thought Susan with certainty as she rode past the dusty shrubbery to the stables. Everyone will be glad to get rid of me for so much of each day.

Of course it'll be dull without Noel, but I expect I shall know some of the others.

Noel, riding down Long Lane to Russet Cottage, felt furious and miserable at the same time. Why did Major Holbrooke have to arrange the dressage course for the very fortnight her family were going away? Why did her father have to lecture on fossils and mummies and Egyptian habits B.C.? She, the only Pony Club member who *really* cared about dressage, was to miss everything; fate was beastly, she decided, and she felt that she hated everyone.

When Christopher had finished letting off steam, by sliding down the banisters, shrieking at the top of his voice and wrestling with both his brothers at once on the hall floor, he got up and, pushing his fair hair, which persisted in being curly despite all his attempts to flatten it with water, out of his eyes, he said, "Of course, I'm not nearly good enough to learn dressage, but I may as well ask old Holbrooke; after all, he can't kill me, can he?"

"He'll probably swear at you and call you a conceited puppy like Sir Charles Dent did at the Boxing Day meet last year," said David.

"Oh, well, I can take it," said Christopher.

Merry Hemlock-Jones, riding quietly home along the road with her reins hanging loosely on Quaver's neck, thought, it might be amusing. After all there's nothing to do at home. It would be nice to escape White's watchful eye and she would be able to wear her new jodhs or perhaps her breeches and boots and the dark blue coat which she kept for horse shows. She saw herself, tall, slim, long-legged and perfectly dressed on Quaver, looking well-bred and beautifully schooled; she imagined them making a half-pass in full view of the admiring Pony Club and an entranced Major Holbrooke. I must get round Daddy, decided Merry.

They must let me go to this, thought Dick Hayward, trotting Crispin along the grass verge of the Gunston road. I can't spend all my life being coached and they wouldn't let me be one of the horse breakers. If I could only learn all about dressage I shall be able to buy a young horse and school him properly. As far as I can see that's the only way I shall ever get another horse for I won't part with you, old man, he thought, patting Crispin. It's a good thing I'm small for my age; it would be frightful if I suddenly shot up.

"But it isn't as though there's a prize or anything," protested June sullenly.

"You never know, the Major might suddenly decide to award one," suggested Mrs. Cresswell, "but apart from that you must do as the others do, my pet, or you'll find yourself left out of things and you know that you wouldn't like that."

"I wouldn't care," said June. "I hate all of them."

"Now don't be silly, my dear," said Mrs. Cresswell, "even if you don't care for them now it will be different when you're older and there are dances and parties. I shall ring up Major Holbrooke to-morrow and ask for full particulars; he must realise that Glory's a valuable mare and can't be turned out with a crowd of common ponies. Mr. Barington-Brown rang up while you were out," Mrs. Cresswell went on. "He's coming to see Wonder to-morrow."

"I hope you asked a good lot for her," said June disagreeably.

"My dear George, you'll ruin their riding," said Colonel Shellbourne to Major Holbrooke, "it's such a pity. They're grand kids and fine little horsemen, but dressage, *dressage,* my dear fellow, it's absurd."

"Now look here, Harry," said Major Holbrooke, "we've had this out before and it doesn't get us anywhere. You've seen some of our children ride to-day and you know most of the others; if you care to come down again at the end of the fortnight's dressage I shall be very pleased and if you don't think that their riding has improved, I shall be very much surprised."

"What's the use of being surprised when the ponies are all behind the bit and the children have turned into a lot of niggling little pokers?" demanded Colonel Shellbourne.

"They won't," said Major Holbrooke.

"Damn it, man," Colonel Shellbourne roared suddenly, "I bet you ten pounds those children don't ride as well when you've finished as they do now."

"Take him on," advised Captain Barton, who was having tea with the Holbrookes. "You'll win."

"I don't often bet," said Major Holbrooke, "but I admit this is tempting. Can you afford to lose a tenner, Harry? And who is to decide whether the children ride better or worse?"

"I shan't lose it," said Colonel Shellbourne, "so you needn't worry about that and, tell you what, George, there are some Pony Club hunter trials near my place on Saturday the eighteenth. You bring the kids and their ponies down, I'll put 'em up, and they can enter. It's a nice little course and we'll soon see what your dressage business has done to them. Both of us are man enough to admit it if we're in the wrong?"

"Right you are," said Major Holbrooke.

It was Sunday. A hot, summer Sunday with a breeze which stirred the trees. The sky was clear, bright blue and seemed to promise another fine day to follow; the birds were singing and the bees were busy among the flowers.

Most of the Pony Club members were having tea in their gardens. At the Priory the Radcliffes had laid their table under the big cedar on the lawn and now they were all eating bread, butter and honey and fruit cake and talking with their mouths full. At intervals they leaped to their feet to prevent Andrew, who wasn't quite a year old, from eating a daisy or pulling the tails of Roly and Poly, their dachshunds.

"I've only got to whiten the lining of Northwind's saddle now," said Hilary, "and then I'm ready, except for cleaning my shoes and brushing my crash cap."

"Oh lord, I'd forgotten my shoes," said Roger, "and Sky Pilot's saddle isn't nearly clean yet, at least not by the Folly Court standard."

"Gosh," said Evelyn, "what a fuss about a few days of dreary dressage."

"I'm sure you don't want the name of Radcliffe disgraced by dirty tack," said Hilary. "It'll be quite peaceful once we've got the ponies at Folly Court."

"I don't know so much about that," said Roger, "there won't be any frenzied tack cleaning, but what about the bicycles? You know what beasts they are."

"Margaret, there's a perfectly good jam spoon," said Dr. Radcliffe, noticing that his youngest daughter was helping herself to jam with her own knife.

"It only makes more washing up," said Margaret crossly, as she used the spoon.

"I must say I think it's extremely good of your Major Holbrooke to put up all these ponies," said Dr. Radcliffe. "I only hope he knows what he's letting himself in for when he undertakes to have a crowd of children there all day."

"He ought to," said Mrs. Radcliffe, who, like her children, had red hair, "after all, he's got three sons."

"He's probably forgotten what they were like as children," said the Doctor, "but anyway," he went on, looking at Roger and Hilary, "do try to behave and don't treat his garden as you do this one."

"I *do* wish I could go," said James.

" 'Ware Andrew," shrieked Mrs. Radcliffe, "he's eating gravel."

The Hemlock-Jones's lawn was much tidier than the Radcliffes.

There were no daisies growing in the bright green turf, because the Brigadier employed a first-class gardener and daisies were ruthlessly pulled up or poisoned with weed-killer wherever they appeared. Their tea table was much tidier too; it hadn't been inefficiently laid by Marga and James with all the knives on the left side, no one had spilt the milk or dropped the honey spoon, no one thought of talking with his mouth full. Merry sat between her mother who was tall, grey-haired and gracious—the sort of person who opens bazaars and sits on committees—and a friend of her father's, who had come to tea. The Brigadier asked Mr. Bransome, "Do you know that mad fellow, Holbrooke?"

"George Holbrooke, the Master of the West Barsetshire, do you mean?"

"Had a very good war, and all that," said the Brigadier, "but he's not quite my line of country. He's mad keen on this Pony Club business and now he's running a dressage course, whatever that may be."

"I'm *so* looking forward to it," said Merry enthusiastically. "I'm sure it's going to be *wonderful* fun."

"I do hope that a sandwich luncheon every day won't give you indigestion, darling," said her mother.

"I've told White to pack up a huge parcel of things for Quaver," said Merry, "and he's marked all his brushes so that they can't be muddled up with any one else's. I'm taking both his double bridle and snaffle, two martingales and a pair of overreach boots as well as all the usual rugs and bandages."

Fenchurch House, square, solid and built in grey stone, had a very small garden with a tiny lawn, on which the Minton family were having tea. Because Fenchurch was a long way from Folly Court, Mrs. Holbrooke had asked Christopher to stay during the course and he felt slightly nervous and was wondering how he was going to keep up his best manners for a fortnight.

"Look, you'd better take my riding stick; it's in better repair than yours," said David, and Martin offered to lend Christopher his best tie—a green one, covered in tiny galloping horses. "You've a clean shirt for every other day," said Mrs. Minton, "two very decayed ones for emergencies and your best white shirt for the hunter trials."

"Now, mind you behave yourself, Christopher," said Mr. Minton. "Don't bolt your food or slide down the banisters, don't shriek or slam doors. Remember to say thank you, call Major Holbrooke sir and open doors for ladies."

"I shall never remember all that," said Christopher.

"Now, remember to ring up if you need anything," said Mrs. Minton, "and mind you tell Mrs. Holbrooke if you feel ill."

Mrs. Barington-Brown didn't approve of tea in the garden. She thought that wasps stung one, caterpillars crawled on one and nameless insects fell into the jam, so Susan and Noel, who was staying at The Towers, for her parents had already started on their lecture tour, sat in the lounge with plates and cups and saucers perched perilously on their knees or the arms of their chairs.

"I do hope I'm sensible to ride Wonder," said Susan.

"It'll be awful if she goes badly; everyone will know that it's my fault, but poor Beauty will be worn out if she has to carry me every day."

"June will be pleased if Wonder doesn't go properly," said Noel, "but still you'll get expert advice from the Major."

"You'll have to behave at Folly Court," said Susan. "No upsetting the milk; I'm glad it's not me, I can't keep my best manners up for a whole day, much less fourteen."

"You should be ashamed, Susan," said Mrs. Barington-Brown.

"Your manners are much better than mine, Susan," said Noel.

"Oh, they're not," answered Susan. "I can't make conversation at all."

"Well, you don't spill things or forget to supply your neighbour with food like I do," said Noel.

"I wonder who are the other members staying at Folly Court?" said Susan. "They must be people from the Gunston direction, I should think, but not Dick; he's coming over each day, he told me."

At Dormers, the Cresswell's modernised Elizabethan cottage, the rustic garden furniture was tidily arranged on the crazy paving and the chocolate biscuits and the little iced cakes were melting in the sunshine. Mrs. Cresswell was telephoning. June picked the bark off the garden seat until her curiosity became too much for her and then she stood in the cottage doorway and tried to gather what her mother's conversation was about.

She realised that her mother was talking to Major Holbrooke and she scowled, for she had no wish to go on the dressage course. "What did he want?" she asked sullenly when her mother had finished.

"Just to settle everything," said Mrs. Cresswell. "I've at

last made him realise that Glory's a valuable mare and cannot be turned out with other animals or in a strange field. He offered a loose-box, but he said that he had made it a condition of the course that everyone was to be responsible for their own mount, that meant that you would have to clean out her stable, which I told him was out of the question."

"I should jolly well hope so," said June. "What does he think Wilson's paid for?"

"Well, it's all settled now, dear," said Mrs. Cresswell. "I'm going to drive you and Glory over in the trailer each morning—she's to have a loose-box at lunchtime and I'm going to fetch you back in the evening."

"What a lot of bother for some silly dressage, which I know already," said June ungraciously. "Honestly, Mummy, you are a fool."

"Really, June, what a way to speak to your mother," said Mrs. Cresswell sharply. "I buy you an expensive animal and this is all the return I get; unless you take more trouble you'll find that Barington-Brown child beating you on Wonder, then you'll look a fool having your new animal beaten by the one that you've sold."

Dick skipped tea because his parents had visitors. He loathed visitors, or at least the smart ones which his parents invited down from London nearly every week-end. They always made the mistake of treating him as though he was twelve and then, when they heard his real age, they looked at him pityingly—or so he imagined. Now it was time to turn Crispin out, and he walked down to the stable with his hands in his pockets whistling softly to himself. Since his parents had agreed to his going on the dressage course, Dick had been giving Crispin two feeds of oats and an extra good groom every day. It was worth it, he thought. He sat on the gate for a little and watched Crispin grazing under the slanting evening sun. He admired the pony's shining, dark brown coat, his black points, one white sock and the crooked race down his forehead. Not for all the smart show horses in the world, thought Dick, would he part with Crispin.

John Manners, hot, dusty and tired, grabbed a bucket of corn and began to fling it round the farmyard for the hens and ducks, which came tearing in from the neighbouring fields. He had spent the whole afternoon helping his father to cart straw bales. It was the least he could do, he thought, considering that he was going away for the next fortnight, but now it was five o'clock and he still had to have tea, pack, feed the dogs, clean his shoes and Turpin's tack and shut up the hens. He would never be ready, he thought despondently; how *could* he be ready to start for Folly Court at nine next morning? He fetched his tack from the stable; the new double bridle was still very stiff; his saddle looked disgracefully dirty; it was nearly a fortnight since he had cleaned it.

"Tea, John," called his mother from the garden.

"Hurry up and wash, John," shouted his father from the hall. "Coming," answered John crossly. But at tea his mother said, "I've done most of your packing, John. Your father's lending you his revelation suitcase—it's smarter than the one you take to school—and I've made the dogs' dinners because I felt sure that you'd be in a hurry."

"Thanks awfully, Mum," said John, feeling as though a load had been lifted from his mind.

"It's a bit much," said Henry Thornton, "to make me share a room with this John what's-his-name and not to tell me what he's like. Come on, Aunt Carol, allay my fears. I asked Uncle George, but he only looked at me disapprovingly and said that it would do me good to share a room. I'm sure John's tough. Does he sleep with his window open top and bottom, whatever the weather and wake one at dawn with hearty advice about cold baths?"

"To tell you the truth," said Mrs. Holbrooke, putting down the *Sunday Times*, "I don't know very much about him. But he's a year younger than you so you ought to be able to shut him up and by the time your uncle has finished teaching you dressage you'll all be so exhausted that you won't want to talk."

"Oh, Aunt, you do sound grim," said Henry. "Is Uncle George becoming one of those people who disapprove of the younger generation? You know, 'gone to the dogs, what?' and all the rest of it. I bet he is. I felt sure he had an ulterior motive in running a dressage course; he's trying to do us good—to toughen us up. If there's anything I dislike it's things that are good for me and if there's one thing I'll never be, it's tough."

"Henry, you talk too much," said his aunt with a smile. "And don't worry about your uncle's opinion of your character; he won't mind what you do if you ride well."

CHAPTER THREE

Confusion had reigned in the stable yard at Folly Court since nine o'clock. Blake, the Major's stud groom, had been trying to restore order, but now he had been captured by Mrs. Cresswell, who was telling him Golden Glory's pedigree complete with a detailed account of what prizes and races her many half-brothers and sisters had won. Whenever Blake tried to say anything she interrupted him with shrill cries to June to move Glory away from the other horses' heels. Fred and Victor—the under grooms—were each holding several ponies, which had been deserted by their owners; half the Pony Club members were asking each other where they were supposed to put their head collars and grooming tools and the other half were arguing with their parents as to whether they really needed their hard hats, mackintoshes and martingales.

"No, not the martingale, Daddy," said Susan. "I can't help what Mrs. Cresswell says about jumping Wonder in one, I know the Major disapproves of them."

Henry Thornton had been told to show the Pony Club members the temporary saddle room, where they were to keep their tack and grooming tools, but he had forgotten where it was and he was wandering about looking for it. Major and Mrs. Holbrooke were making polite conversation to the parents of the members who were staying at the Court; to Mrs. Minton and Colonel Manners and Mr. Barington-Brown, who had brought Noel's luggage.

At last everything was sorted out; the parents drove home, the grooms went back to their work. Mrs. Holbrooke walked down to the aviary to visit her famous collection of rare birds and the Pony Club members filed into the paddock. They were rather disappointed when they saw the usual school marked out with four white posts; they had all been expecting something special and June had hoped for a proper arena; she felt certain that she knew more about dressage than any of the other members and she had pictured herself half passing from "B" to "F" while they all tied themselves in knots.

"Now, this morning," said Major Holbrooke, when everyone was in the school, "we are going to revise what you have already learned and make sure that you are all sitting correctly, for without a correct seat all the teaching of the next few days will be wasted. Roger," he went on, "will you lead round the school, please?"

June was annoyed; she felt that she should have been asked to lead, but she took second place and made Golden Glory walk as fast as she could, hoping to overtake Roger and Sky Pilot. Merry pouted; she, too, had wanted to lead; now, she thought, Quaver would jog and pull. "Walk, Quaver," she said sharply as she followed June. Henry Thornton, long-legged and lank, was riding his uncle's Black Magic, a good looking thoroughbred, coal black except for a small neat star on her forehead. Noel followed Dick and behind her rode Hilary and Susan. Christopher, feeling a little bashful because everyone seemed to know so much more than he did, was last but one, and John, still hot and bothered from the whirl of preparation, brought up the rear. Well, I'm here, he thought, no more hurry for a fortnight.

"Prepare to trot, trot on," said Major Holbrooke. Sky Pilot, another black but with a crooked blaze and three white socks, was a sensible type of horse and he trotted on steadily, but Glory swished her tail, lay back her ears and then reluctantly obeyed a sharp kick from June's outside heel—the one the Major couldn't see. Quaver, tired of Merry's nagging hands, threw his head about and pulled. Black Magic, who was very fit and had spent Sunday in the stable, gave a couple of light-hearted bucks and, at the back of the line, Christopher was having his arms pulled out by Fireworks. Presently the Major gave the order to canter. Black Magic bucked again, but Henry, who had been riding for ten years, wasn't unseated; Glory was cantering too slowly for the other horses and ponies so, led by Henry, they passed her and cantered on after Roger and Merry, except for Fireworks. He increased his pace until he was galloping flat out round the field with Christopher tugging frantically at the reins and the Major shouting at him to sit down in his saddle. The other members pulled up to watch and, after galloping round the field three or four times, Fireworks began to tire; at last he consented to pull up. "Whew, you are an old devil," said Christopher, trotting back to the school.

"That pony's a menace," said the Major, "does he often behave like that?"

"Well, yes, sometimes," answered Christopher, "but he's worse to-day because I gave him a good feed of oats last night."

"Someone seems to have hotted him up very thoroughly," said the Major. "He's quite a young pony, isn't he?"

"Six," answered Christopher.

"I should imagine that his breaker took him out hunting, or entered him for gymkhanas too early," said the Major. "That's how most horses and ponies are spoiled; simply because their trainers are in too much of a hurry. Still, he's a nice-looking pony and I should think he can jump. We must see what we can do with him. I expect that when you were galloping round the field just now you thought that you were doing your utmost to stop him, didn't you?"

"Well, yes, I did," answered Christopher. "I don't see how I could have pulled any harder."

"Actually," said the Major, "you weren't pulling very hard at all, because first you pulled yourself out of the saddle and then you rested your hands on your pony's withers to regain your balance before having another tug at the reins. Well now, that may seem a clear aid to you, but it doesn't seem so to the pony. The first thing you have to do is to strengthen your seat and then you will be able to go on saying 'stop', until your pony obeys. And remember that a correct seat is a strong seat and that the leg position is the key to the seat. Now walk round the school everyone, I'm going to have a look at those seats." Everyone sat up very straight and began to try to arrange himself into what he hoped was the correct position, but in spite of this the Major found plenty of faults to correct.

The Radcliffes and John Manners all had their legs a little too far forward; Merry was sitting in the back of her saddle with her legs much too far forward and her toes down. The Major told her that she was behind her horse's centre of gravity and quite unable to use her legs; but, as soon as he turned to look at Henry, Merry pouted and returned to her usual position. Henry's fault was that his leg position was too fluid; "Sit a little farther forward in your saddle, now draw your lower leg back and at the same time push down your knees and heels hard. Now, there we have the correct leg position," said Major Holbrooke to the other members, "a pointed knee, the heel down and the toe just behind a vertical line from the knee to the ground. If you really concentrate on getting the leg position, it will become second nature to you in a very few days, but if you wait hopefully for a miracle or for me to nag you into position, you'll be indifferent riders for the rest of your lives.

"Now, come on, June," the Major went on in tones of exasperation, "surely I've told you the correct seat often enough. The way you sit may be all right for the show ring, but it's useless for dressage; you can't use your hands if they're in your stomach, you can't use your legs if they're too far forward." Susan and Dick had no glaring faults, but Noel was told to look up, not at the ground, and Christopher, though his leg position was quite good, sat too far forward and held his reins too short.

Having corrected everyone, the Major looked up the line again. The Radcliffes were telling John about Richard Morrison's birthday party, Noel was looking at the ground, Merry and June were back in their old positions; it was disheartening, thought Major Holbrooke, but he would see if he could wake them up a bit. He gave the order to trot on, with the riders sitting down instead of rising and to change the rein, and, when they were trotting round the school in the opposite direction, he told them to prepare, and then, to halt. Some of the members, those who had been taught by the Major before, knew that they should use their legs when they halted, but others like Merry and Henry just pulled on the reins. The Major explained the importance of using the legs when halting and he also told Christopher that he must open his fingers and relax his hands a moment before Fireworks actually obeyed his aid to stop.

The members practised halting from the walk and trot and when everyone was able to do this reasonably well, the Major told them to cross their stirrups. John and Christopher made rueful faces, for their ponies had uncomfortable trots, but they suffered less than Henry and Merry, who weren't used to riding without stirrups and who soon began to groan and gasp. When they were told to walk they sighed with relief, but not for long, the next order was to trot, holding their reins in their outside hands and, when the Major gave the order, they had to touch their inside toes with their inside hands. Merry, Henry and

June felt that this was rather beneath their dignity but Susan and Christopher were laughing so much that they were in danger of falling off. Then they practised reining back.

Fireworks was hopeless; he stuck his head in the air, put all his weight on his haunches and then said that he couldn't possibly go backwards. But, by making him face a fence, he was persuaded to back two grudging little steps, for which he was rewarded by a great many pats. Noel couldn't make Sonnet back straight, which, she was told, was disgraceful, considering that she had been schooling her for the last nine months. Henry and Merry had no idea that you were supposed to use your legs and June got a lecture because she knew that you should use them but, according to the Major, she was too lazy to put them in the proper place to do so.

After halting and reining back several times from both the walk and trot they practised turns on the forehand and then the Major said that there was just time for a few jumps before lunch. Everyone, except Merry, was delighted.

"Hurray," said John.

"Oh goody," exclaimed Susan.

"About time too," grumbled Roger Radcliffe.

"Don't you think that the ground is rather hard?" Merry asked June in a troubled voice. "I must speak to Major Holbrooke; I don't want Quaver's legs ruined." She rode across to where the Major was beginning to move jumps from the pile by the gate. Dick, Roger and John gave their horses to the other members to hold and ran to help him. "Oh, Major Holbrooke," began Merry, "don't you think the ground's rather hard? I don't usually jump Quaver at all in the summer, you see he wins quite a lot in hunter classes and I'm anxious not to spoil his legs. I mean the slightest thing wrong with their legs puts them right out of the 'money', doesn't it?"

"I don't think you need worry," answered the Major patiently, "the going's very good at the moment and we're not going to jump at all high."

"I see; well, I suppose it's all right then, but it would be so tragic if he went lame." The Major remained silent, so Merry turned and rode back to the others.

"What did he say?" asked June.

"He seems to think it'll be all right," answered Merry.

"The trouble about the Major," said June, "is that he doesn't know how valuable horses ought to be treated. No one but a fool would lend Black Magic to that silly Henry; why she's won three light-weight hunter classes already this year. And look how he hunts them—tearing through woods and along roads as though they were a lot of common old screws instead of show horses. No one in their senses would treat valuable horses like that."

"Of course I hunt Quaver, but he's quite unstoppable and completely tireless, but I never show jump him and I always insist that White puts exercise bandages on if the going's hard. I must put them on you to-morrow, Quaver."

"I shall tell Wilson to put Glory's on too," said June, "I don't want her blemished."

"Now," said Major Holbrooke, when the jumps were ready, "four very small fences, but don't be misled, they're not quite as easy as they look. They're purposely arranged out of line, so that you'll have to use your legs and reins to keep your horses balanced and to straighten them out between each fence. Roger, you first, please."

Roger jumped the first two, but he let Sky Pilot run out of the third fence.

"He used his legs," said Major Holbrooke, "but, as I expect you all noticed, he didn't keep contact with his horse's mouth. Try again." Roger managed to clear all four fences at his second attempt and Henry, who followed him, cleared them at his first, but the Major said that it was because he had an obliging horse and that Henry's riding had been horrible to behold; he was to keep his heels down, his legs back and his knees in. Hilary cleared all the jumps on the stout blue roan, Northwind, who was a sticky jumper. The Major said that she had used her legs very well, but that if Northwind had been a hot pony, she would have found her reins too long to keep him straight.

Merry jumped the first jump with the backward seat and allowed Quaver to run out of the second; whereupon the Major pointed out that if she persisted in riding with her present impracticable seat, she could neither put her weight in her stirrups nor use her legs. Merry tried again; she jumped the first fence in better style, but she still let Quaver run out at the second. "You didn't use your legs at all," the Major told her, "it is no use sitting there and hoping for the best; directly you land over one fence, use your legs and ride your horse at the next." The third try was more successful; Merry used her legs and Quaver jumped the second fence, but she rolled off over his shoulder. The Major asked if she was all right and, getting slowly to her feet, she replied rather crossly that she supposed so, but she grumbled to Noel and Susan that her back hurt and that the Major was a fool to expect a horse that wasn't a show jumper to jump fences which weren't in a straight line.

Meanwhile Dick jumped all the fences very well, except that he looked down all the way, and John cleared them, but in what the Major described a "rough and ready style". "You lost contact with his mouth so you had to haul him round to jump the third bar; did you feel it?" asked Major Holbrooke. John agreed that he had. It was June's turn next and riding as usual with her reins too long and her legs too far forward, she found herself in difficulties with Golden Glory, who napped towards the other horses, running backwards and swinging round whenever June tried to ride her at the jumps. The Major shouted instructions. June was to shorten her reins, to use her legs and stick. After some delay Glory approached the first fence, but it was a long time before she could be persuaded to jump all four fences and both the Major and June were hot and cross.

I'm sure to do it all wrong, thought Noel as she rode at the jumps; Sonnet didn't try to run out or refuse it is true, but she jumped lazily and knocked down the last pole. The Major said that it was disgraceful, that after nine months of schooling, Noel still hadn't got her going in a balanced manner.

Noel told herself that her riding was becoming worse instead of better and that being the champion horse breaker must have made her conceited and this was the dismal result. Meanwhile Susan was being lectured, for Golden Wonder had thrown up her head and taken the jumps far too fast and completely out of control. When the Major inquired why she wasn't wearing her usual standing martingale, Susan replied that she had made Daddy take it home because she knew that he, the Major, disapproved of them. The Major, already hot and tired, exploded with wrath. He objected to being told that he disapproved of standing martingales when he used them frequently on young and spoiled horses. They were quite out of place on a finished horse and, of course, in the show ring, but to cast aside your martingale without first having cured the fault which had made it necessary, was ridiculous. Having dealt with Susan, the Major turned to Christopher. Fireworks, awaiting his turn, was already wild with excitement. Major Holbrooke gave him one look and then separated one jump from the rest, lowering it until it was only a few inches in height. He told Christopher to circle at the walk in front of the jump until Fireworks stopped expecting to jump it. At first he danced and jogged and pulled but, after a while he became bored and walked quietly; then the Major told Christopher to walk him over the jump, circle round and walk over again. By the time Fireworks had walked over the tiny jump twelve times, he was walking quietly, with his neck stretched out, on a loose rein. This, the Major told Christopher, was what they wanted. "And now," he added, "it is time for lunch."

Lunch, for the Pony Club members who were staying at Folly Court, was an uncomfortable meal. John was never very good at conversation, at Lower Basset Farm no one talked much except about the animals or the weather; sometimes the colonel would discourse on the iniquities of the Government, or the stupidity of the other members of his golf club, but Mrs. Manners always agreed with him in a soothing voice and John fidgeted or thought of something else, so it could hardly be called conversation. Christopher usually had plenty to say for himself, but now he was afraid of upsetting his glass of water or using the wrong knife and fork, so he concentrated on his table manners and only spoke when he was spoken to.

Noel, who was normally rather a good conversationalist, was feeling depressed because the Major had said that her schooling of Sonnet was disgraceful and Henry, who had decided that the Pony Club members were dull and that the next fortnight was going to be frightful, would only talk to his uncle and aunt.

Major and Mrs. Holbrooke made frantic efforts to break the silence; they asked where each person went to school and whether they liked it and the length of their summer holidays. Mrs. Holbrooke talked about dogs to Christopher and the Major tried to talk to John about tractors, but everyone was glad when the meal was over and Mrs. Holbrooke said that the grown-ups were going to have coffee in the garden but Henry could show the members their rooms. Henry said that he wanted coffee, but his uncle told him that he could have it afterwards, so, grumbling and muttering he led the way up the broad staircase and along a short corridor hung with portraits.

"Gosh," said Christopher, whose spirits were rising now that he had left the dining-room. "Are they relations of yours, Henry?"

"Yes, they're my ancestors," answered Henry.

"She looks fierce," said John, pointing at an elderly lady dressed in early Victorian clothes.

"No wonder you look like you do," said Christopher, "I mean no one could help it with relations like this."

"You're a cheeky devil," said Henry. "This is our room, John," he went on, opening the door. "It used to belong to my cousins."

"Oh good," said John, "it looks out towards the stables."

"That's your bed by the window," said Henry. "I've tried them and they're both hard, but I think the one I've bagged is slightly better."

"Trust you," said John.

"Noel, you've got one of the proper spare rooms; here." He led the way across the passage. It was a large room and it looked too elegant and tidy as spare bedrooms have a habit of doing. The windows looked across to Folly Farm and Noel could see the field in which the six New Forest ponies had been turned out the first time she saw them.

"I'm sorry for you, Noel," said Christopher; "one couldn't have a riot in here without busting something."

"Never mind," said Noel. "I like green and white rooms and I've got a marvellous view."

"This is our sitting-room," said Henry, opening a door at the end of the corridor. "It was my cousins'. You've all got to come in here if you want to make a row and, incidentally, there are quite a lot of books for those with childish tastes."

"Hark at Grandpa!" said Christopher.

"Oh, shut up," said Henry.

"Well, you did sound rather superior," objected Noel.

"I am," answered Henry.

"Cut it out," said John.

"Where's my bedroom?" asked Christopher.

"You've got Cousin David's room," Henry told him, "though personally, I think the broom cupboard's more in your line. No disturbance allowed in the passages," he added, when Christopher rushed at him. "Here you are; David's the artist and when he ran out of canvas he used his bedroom walls."

"Gosh," said Christopher.

"You are lucky," said Noel. "I wish that I had this room." On one wall there was a hunting scene; above the bed an Irish landscape; beside the door a still life—apples and oranges on a dish and a bottle of wine—and between the windows a Shire horse drawing a hay wagon.

"I don't know so much about that," said Henry. "I should think they become overpowering after a few weeks. It's odd that Uncle George should have an artistic son; I mean he doesn't seem quite the type. But perhaps David took after Aunt Carol; anyway he's becoming quite famous as a sporting artist."

"Well, these look awfully good," said John.

"My dear John, not *good*," objected Henry. "If you can't say anything more professional about a picture you should just stand spellbound with your mouth shut."

"I don't see why I shouldn't say what I like," answered John, flushing with anger.

"It's a free country," said Noel.

"Of course you can say what you like," answered Henry, "but you'll only make your average mentality seem lower than ever."

"Oh shut up," said John, in exasperated accents.

"That's what the man in the street always says when he

hears something that he doesn't understand," said Henry, "don't you agree, Noel?"

"I think you're trying to be irritating," said Noel. "Hadn't you better go and drink your coffee before it gets any colder?"

"Oh all right," said Henry, "identify yourself with the man in the street. But you won't get rid of me for long; we've all got to clean tack."

"I'm going to put on my disreputable slacks," said Noel, as Henry ran downstairs. "I brought them for tack cleaning."

"I'm going to change too," said Christopher. "I'm much too hot in jodhs."

"Fancy having to share a room with that affected idiot," said John. "I do think it's unfair. Why couldn't they have put you in with him, Christopher, or let us share a room, that wouldn't have been so bad."

"Thanks for the compliment," said Christopher.

The Pony Club members, who were coming over to Folly Court each day, had eaten their lunches lying in the shade of the oak trees in the park. June and Merry were a little way from the others. As they ate their egg sandwiches, they had pulled Major Holbrooke's teaching to pieces; during the biscuit and cake stage they had capped each other's stories of their horses amusing habits and now they were discussing the iniquities of their grooms.

"So I said, 'You've got to, otherwise I shall speak to Daddy,' and that finished it," said Merry.

"Well, Wilson . . ." began June, but she was interrupted by Christopher. "Come on, you lazy devils," he said. "You've got to clean your tack. Henry's fetching the hot water and we can watch the Major jumping Gay Crusader at half-past three if we've finished the tack by then."

"How terribly interesting," said Merry sarcastically.

Some of the members had brought their own tack cleaning outfits and Blake had provided a number of sponges, dusters and a couple of tins of saddle soap for those who hadn't, but there was only one saddle horse and that soon began to cause trouble, because everyone wanted to clean his saddle first and the horse could only hold five.

"Well, I don't really mind," said Noel. "I'll clean my bridle first."

"So will I," said Susan. "I'm sure I don't care which I do."

"I don't care either way," said Christopher.

"It certainly won't alter the fate of nations," said Dick, starting on his bridle.

"I don't know about that," said Henry; "this is the way dictatorships begin; a picking up of unconsidered trifles; a little quiet shoving and, suddenly, you find that you're being ruled by someone you despise."

"Well, I put my saddle on first and I don't see why *I* should be pushed out; in fact I'm definitely not going to be," said Merry and she pushed at Hilary's saddle, which infuriated Hilary and made her even more obstinate. Roger muttered something about June and Merry trying to run the whole show and Henry told John that he was the youngest and must make room for his elders and betters.

"I'm not younger than Hilary," answered John angrily, "you can take your own beastly saddle off."

"Why not toss up?" suggested Noel hastily.

"Oh, come on, John," said Dick, "join the bridle brigade —it's far more select."

"All right, I suppose I may as well; but you needn't think I'm going to give in every time."

"No, of course not," said Dick tactfully, "we must arrange something; we five might begin with saddles to-morrow."

"But I just can't bear cleaning my bridle first, I *never* do," said Merry.

"It would do you good then," said Christopher.

"Why, may I inquire?" asked Merry.

"Because it's bad for you always to have your own way," answered Christopher.

"You're simply being rude and impertinent, and that's my saddle soap sponge you're using," said Merry, leaning over the saddle horse and making a snatch at it.

"Ask nicely," said Christopher, dodging away.

"How dare you borrow it without asking?" stormed Merry.

"I didn't even know it was yours," answered Christopher.

"Well, give it back at once," said Merry.

"Not likely. You ask for it properly," answered Christopher.

Merry rushed at him, tripped over the tack bucket and cursing loudly, pursued him out into the yard.

"Gone away!" yelled Roger.

"Yoicks, tally ho, get on to him!" shouted Hilary.

"What a filthy mess," grumbled Henry. "Well, it's somebody else's turn to fetch the water."

Christopher dodged round the grass plot in the middle of the yard, dashed in and out of the forage room, round the barn and finally climbed on the top of the muck heap, where Merry, still wearing her best jodhs, had no wish to follow him.

"You wait," she threatened, and "You can't stay up there all afternoon—the Major will see you."

Christopher only laughed. "Ask nicely," he said.

Merry became abusive; she told him that he was revolting, and the worst-behaved boy she had ever met. At last Christopher became bored, "If you want your sponge, you'll have to come up and get it," he said and, leaving it on the muck heap, he jumped down and ran back to the saddle room.

The Major was wandering round, glancing at the tack. He said that he wouldn't take on any of the members as grooms even if he was paid to; that he had never seen tack so badly cleaned. Christopher began work on his saddle with tremendous energy, trying to look as though he had been there all the time. A few moments later Merry, furiously angry, stamped in. "Of all the disgusting, revolting, badly behaved boys," she began and then she saw Major Holbrooke and stopped abruptly. "Quarrelling already?" asked the Major. Merry didn't answer; she turned her back on him and began to clean her bridle.

"Not exactly a quarrel," said Dick.

" 'We are but little children weak'," quoted Henry.

After dinner, when dusk lay over Folly Court, peaceful now that most of the Pony Club members had gone home, Noel, Christopher and John collected the Holbrooke dogs and walked down to the fields where the ponies were turned out. It was a lovely night; dark and cool and the clear sky seemed full of stars. The fields lay in shadow waiting for the moon to rise; the grass was wet with dew.

The dogs, two terriers and a spaniel, ran ahead sniffing the tantalising smells of the night air with excitement and breaking the stillness with sharp barks, when they caught sight of an unwary rabbit.

"It's much too nice to go to bed," said Noel.

"I should like to sleep out," said John.

"Coop, coop," called Noel softly for they had reached the field where the three mares—Sonnet, Black Magic and Golden Wonder—were turned out.

Noel stood with one arm round Sonnet's neck as she munched her apple. It was silly to care so much about being good at dressage and successful in shows, thought Noel, what did all that matter in comparison with owning an agreeable grey pony with which one could share the magic of a summer night? "You do smell lovely," she told Sonnet, burying her face in the pony's neck.

"Oh come on, Noel; do stop slopping. I want to see Fireworks," said Christopher.

CHAPTER FOUR

EVERYTHING was grand, thought John, sitting up in bed and pulling back the curtain nearest to him. It was always wonderful to wake up and find that you weren't at school, but this was even better for he wouldn't hear his father's shout in a moment, calling him down, reminding him that he had the puppies and hens to feed, that it was almost breakfast time and that afterwards he was needed to help with harrowing, haymaking, corn cutting or another of the endless jobs on a farm. It was luxury to know that he needn't get up, that there was no hurry and nothing to do but ride. He lay back and thought that, but for Henry, life would be perfect. Not that Henry was being annoying at that moment; he was still sound asleep with the bedclothes over his head.

Noel was awake. She drew back her curtains and thought, another lovely day. The world was gay with colour, clear blue, bright green and yellow sunshine. She determined that to-day she would enjoy herself. She would ride much better than yesterday and when the Major criticised her riding and Sonnet's behaviour, she wouldn't be downcast, for, after all, they had come to learn.

There was a loud bang on her door. "Come in," she called.

"Oh, hallo," said Christopher, peering in, "aren't *you* up yet? I've been trying to get those other lazy devils out of bed, but Henry only groans and John threw a shoe at me. I don't see how anyone can stay in on such a wizard morning; I'm going out."

"What energy," said Noel with a yawn. "Still, I do agree; I'll be out in a moment."

When Noel found Christopher he was helping the grooms by emptying the wheelbarrows and fetching hay and clean straw for the horses. He was also asking a great many questions.

"Oh good, you've come at last," said Christopher. "Blake says that we had better catch all the ponies and give them their feeds, otherwise they won't have digested in time."

"O.K.," said Noel. "I'll get the head collars."

They caught the three mares first and, mounting off the gate, rode up to the stables; Noel on Sonnet leading Black Magic and Christopher on Wonder, who, he said, was a super ride. Then they went back for Crispin, Turpin and Fireworks and finally for Sky Pilot, Quavèr and Northwind. Noel rode Sky Pilot and suggested that Christopher should have Northwind, but he was determined to try Quaver. It took him a long time to scramble on from the gate because Quaver wasn't very obliging about standing still. But at last Christopher managed it and then he insisted on having a canter up the grass verge at the side of the drive. Of course he couldn't pull Quaver up at the end and he tore into the stable yard with a fearful clatter and Noel, following more slowly, was afraid that he would have met the Major or Merry. However John was the only person in the yard and he merely asked Christopher what on earth he thought he was doing, and added that he had come to help feed. They distributed the feeds—oats, bran and chaff—and then, feeling rather gay and very hungry, they tore back to the house at full speed, hoping that it was time for breakfast. The Major was reading *The Times* as he ate his bacon and eggs. He said "Good morning," told the members to help themselves and returned to *The Times*. There was no sign of Henry and they felt rather subdued; they talked in whispers and tried not to disturb the Major. At last, to their relief, Mrs. Holbrooke appeared. She asked if they had all slept all night and told the Major that he was a hopeless host and why hadn't he poured the coffee? He answered that surely Noel could pour the coffee and where was Henry?

When Noel, John and Christopher had finished breakfast they wandered out to the barn to groom their ponies; the Radcliffes were already there, hard at work, and Merry was rushing about in a distracted manner looking for the body brush, which, she said, someone had taken. However John found it in the saddle room, which annoyed her still more.

Susan arrived at a quarter past nine and persuaded Noel, who had finished grooming Sonnet, to do one side of Wonder and tell her all about life at Folly Court. Henry dashed out at twenty minutes to ten and, after a very perfunctory brush, began to saddle Black Magic. The Cresswells rolled up with their trailer just as the Radcliffes, Noel, Susan, John and Christopher were mounting.

"Where are the others?" asked Major Holbrooke as he came into the yard.

"Henry's just coming," answered Christopher. "Merry's in a flat spin about her bandages and Dick hasn't turned up yet."

"But we've groomed Crispin," added John.

"Oh, yes, Dick rang up," said the Major. "His father took the car so he's coming by taxi."

"Shall I go and bridle Crispin then?" asked Noel.

"Yes, you may as well, since we're waiting for the others," answered the Major. By the time that Noel had bridled Crispin and Major Holbrooke had adjusted Wonder's standing martingale, and told Merry to take off all the exercise bandages she had just put on Quaver and which were about to fall off, Dick, looking very hot and angry, had arrived. He apologised several times for being late, but in spite of being told that it was quite all right and hadn't mattered a bit, everyone could see that he was still very upset.

Hilary thought that the Major seemed in rather a bad temper too; he set into Merry and June straight away, telling them that they were sitting just as badly as the day before and that it was impossible to teach dressage to people with incorrect seats or leg positions.

I wonder who is the best rider? thought Susan, not me, any rate. I used to think it was Noel; she always looked good on Romany, but she seems to have got worse since she had Sonnet. Henry doesn't look bad, she thought, except that his toes go down sometimes and, of course, the Radcliffes are good. She glanced up at Roger on tall, black Sky Pilot; he looked different now that he wore glasses; they didn't suit his snub nose and square, freckled face.

John thought that Turpin was nice and fresh to-day. The Major's oats were doing him good; Father never let him have enough at home.

Christopher's crash cap kept falling over his eyes and his arms were already aching from trying to control Fireworks, who seemed worse behaved than ever this morning.

Noel pulled at Sonnet's head. I wish you'd carry it a bit higher, she thought, the Major will say that you're a disgrace in a minute; for goodness' sake put your hocks under you.

"Come into the centre, everyone," said Major Holbrooke, breaking into their thoughts. "It is no use going on as we are; no one is learning anything and the horses are going to sleep. How many oats did you give your pony this morning?" he asked Noel.

"The wooden measure full," she answered.

"And what about yours?" he asked Christopher.

"Fireworks had the same," answered Christopher. "We gave each of the ponies one measure and each of the horses two."

"Bright couple, aren't you?" said the Major. "Well, in future Fireworks is to have no oats—just bran and chaff—and Sonnet can have two measures three times a day and cod liver oil cake, which Blake will give you. Everyone else must consider whether their horses are too fresh or not fresh enough and adjust their feeding accordingly. Northwind will need more than Golden Wonder, Sky Pilot more than Quaver. This schooling is fairly strenuous and we must get them fit for the hunter trials. Now I'm going to send half of you for a quiet hack while I get to work on the other five; you're all equally hopeless at present, but in different ways. I want Dick, Susan, Noel, John and Christopher now; the rest of you go for a quiet ride and I'll take you directly after lunch."

The hacking party looked rather pleased as they rode away.

"I'm glad I'm with you lot and not with those wet drips," said Christopher to Noel.

"You can't call the Radcliffes drips," objected Noel. "They're rather tough and superior and I don't think Henry's bad really; most of his silliness is just put on."

"Well, I wish he'd take it off then," said John with great feeling.

"Now we can get down to it," said the Major. "I'd better explain what we are trying to do. You all sit quite nicely and your legs are more or less in the right place, so the time has come to turn you from passive into active riders. You can always tell an active rider; he mounts a horse and the animal walks away with a long stride, high head carriage and pricked ears, whereas with a passive rider he would dawdle along looking yearningly back at his stable. Yet you don't often see the active rider give an aid and the passive ones expend enormous energy flapping their legs and brandishing their riding sticks. Now the secret of the active rider's effortless control is the use of his thighs, seat bones and back. A passive rider only uses his calves and sometimes, wrongly, his heels.

"An extremely important point in schooling, of which I cannot remind you too often, is that the horse's head carriage is not improved by pulling on the reins. A horse carries his head too low because he is badly balanced, he has too much weight on his forehand; to lighten the forehand we must make him use his hocks and quarters, by the use of our legs, by schoolwork, by riding up and down hills. *Never* by pulling on the reins. Now I'll discuss you each in turn. Noel's feeling a bit disappointed; she did very well with Romany, but that pony had natural balance. The chief difficulty about Sonnet is that she was in very poor condition when Noel was given her and therefore it has needed an extra effort to get her muscles in working order. But now she's in good condition, we're going to give her plenty of oats and Noel has got to ride her with energy; you must push her hind legs under her every moment that you are in the saddle. Now, Christopher," the Major went on without a pause, "your pony's trouble is due to mismanagement. He's learned that by pulling his weight on his forehead he can get away from his rider and, as soon as he is excited, that is what he does. The cure, of course, is don't let him put his weight on his forehand, but, until you've developed a stronger seat, you can't do that. However you will both be improved by halting and reining back, by riding the school figures and plenty of circling—in fact any exercise which makes him use his hind legs and you your seat.

"The same exercises are also useful for Wonder. Her fault of stargazing, instead of giving her lower jaw to the bit, is due to being ridden by hands instead of legs. Horses that are ridden by people with their legs too far forward invariably acquire bad habits. A light-necked pony tends to stargaze, a heavy-shouldered or less well-balanced one to bore.

"For Turpin and Crispin," the Major went on, "I have the greatest admiration. They are both well-mannered ponies, which know their jobs, but their owners are inclined to take advantage of this and ride them as if they were a mere means of conveyance. Now a great many people would say, why not? But, apart from being a much better ride, a horse which collects is far safer to ride on a slippery road, through woods or among rabbit holes; he is balanced, alert and responsive to the aids. Then in the hunting field you sometimes meet a narrow jump—probably a stile—in a wire fence. 'A very dangerous jump' say all the people on half-schooled horses. And they are quite right; because however wise and sensible their horses may be it is a little nerve-racking to have to place implicit trust in them. But those people who can collect their horses feel quite confident, for they can ride at the fence knowing that their horse is in a position to obey the slightest aid from leg or rein. Now trot on round the school, sitting down. Remember that when you're rising you can't use your seat properly."

They passed a busy and exhausting hour. First they practised halting and turning and from the trot and then they attempted the same work at the canter. It took a great deal of energy on the part of the Major to convince the members that, if they used their seat bones, they could canter from the walk, without even one stride at the trot, and walk again after a certain number of strides. Wonder soon began to go very well indeed and carried her head in the right place instead of stargazing. Turpin and Crispin were no disgrace, but they still lacked impulsion, and

Fireworks' outbursts were becoming less frequent. To Susan and John, Sonnet showed no improvement, but Noel could feel a little more power in her quarters and a corresponding lightening of her forehand, so she was quite content.

"An interesting morning," said Dick as they rode into the yard. "It's more fun with only five of us."

"You're telling me," said Christopher.

"My legs ache," said Noel, dismounting.

"So do mine," said Susan.

"And mine," added Dick.

"That's a good sign," said Major Holbrooke, who had followed them in; "your thighs will ache like anything if you've been doing any work."

"We had a terrific ride," said Roger, when the Major had gone into the house. "We jumped seven hedges, a stile and some posts and rails."

"It was super," said Hilary.

"That's what you call a quiet ride," said Christopher.

"Oh, Lord!" exclaimed Roger. "I forgot that it was meant to be quiet. Are we going to have a fearfully exhausting afternoon?"

"We had a pretty gruelling time this morning," John told him, "but I think that it was harder on us than the ponies."

"I'm going to give Northwind some extra oats," said Hilary.

After lunch the hacking party saw the schooling people into the paddock before setting out on their ride. It was rather hot so they rode in a leisurely manner and chose a wooded way, which Dick knew. It was cool in the bottom of the wood, sheltered from the sun by tangled boughs and it was pleasant to canter up the grass track between the pines, which smelled even stronger than pines usually smell. They wandered homewards down a lane with tall hazel hedges, which met over their heads. They felt lazy, peaceful and contented when they reached Folly Court, hardly in the mood for the bustle of the stable yard or the noisy scramble of tack cleaning. The other members had just come in from the paddock. "We're in a state of collapse," said Hilary.

"We've had a simply ghastly afternoon," said Roger.

"My legs are absolute agony," complained Henry.

"That man's got a terrible temper," said Merry darkly; "you should have heard him flare up."

"To hear you people talk would make anyone think you didn't want to learn dressage," said John.

"Is there any reason to suppose that we do?" asked Merry.

"Uncle G. is all very well," said Henry, "but sometimes he goes too far."

"Yes, he does," agreed June.

"You are an ungrateful lot," said Noel.

"If I were the Major, I wouldn't bother with them," said John angrily. "They're nothing but a discontented lot of grumblers."

"Hark to the man in the street," said Henry. "But you're not the Major and if grumblers are discontented it must be because they've nothing to grumble about. You should always consider the accuracy of your statements before making them, my dear boy."

"Oh shut up," said John. "You think you're frightfully clever, but really you're nothing but a conceited ape."

"Steady on, John," said Dick.

"You mustn't deprive him of his freedom of speech," objected Henry. "After all he can't think so he must talk."

"If you don't shut up, I'll shut you up," said John furiously.

"Now don't be silly," said Dick, putting himself between them.

"My dear Dick, I haven't the slightest intention of fighting him," said Henry, "it would be beneath my dignity."

"Oh, you boys," said Susan, "for goodness' sake stop quarrelling."

"It's four o'clock," said Hilary, looking at her watch, "and I'm sure I can hear your trailer coming, June."

"Oh heavens! It isn't four yet, not really, is it?" shrieked Merry. "I'm not nearly ready and I told White to be punctual because I'm going to a cocktail party. I've got to change. Oh, get out of my way, Christopher," and she began to rush about the saddle room collecting up her possessions.

"How are we going to keep the peace to-night?" Noel asked Christopher as they walked in to tea. "I do wish that Dick was staying."

"I expect that it will blow over," said Christopher optimistically. But the unpleasantness didn't blow over. John wouldn't speak to Henry between tea and dinner and then at dinner Henry took advantage of the presence of the Holbrookes to ask him dozens of questions, which, of course, he had to answer in a reasonably civil manner.

Noel was hoping that Henry would stay downstairs with the Holbrookes, but she was disappointed; after dinner he fetched his coffee and brought it up to the nursery. "I've come to see you behave yourselves," he said, as he followed the Pony Club members in.

"Oh go to the devil," said John, seizing a book at random and sitting down on the sofa.

"Yes, come off it, Henry," said Christopher. "We're getting fed up with you."

"Well, I was fed up with you before you even came," said Henry. "I wouldn't have come to stay if Uncle George had told me that the place was going to be lousy with subnormal Pony Club members."

"Shut up," said Noel quite agreeably. "You're simply trying to irritate."

"Sorry," said Henry. "I forgot that John could understand words of more than one syllable."

John, exasperated beyond endurance, hurled the book he was reading at Henry; unfortunately it missed.

"Oh well *played*," shrieked Henry. John lost his temper completely. He shot across the room and hit Henry as hard as he could. The blow hurt, so Henry lost his temper too and they went for each other, boxing and wrestling in the wildest manner.

"Oh for goodness' sake," said Noel.

"It's no good," said Christopher, "you can't stop them now; we'd better let them have it out; they may feel better afterwards."

So Noel stood by, feeling very ineffective, while Christopher gave John advice and encouragement. Chairs were overturned, books and the bagatelle board fell from the table with a crash, but no-one paid much attention; they had all forgotten they were guests in someone else's house. John and Henry were rolling on the floor still hitting each other as hard as they could when the door opened and the Major appeared.

"Lawks, cave," muttered Christopher in a dismayed voice. Noel felt herself turning scarlet. The Major surveyed the scene. "Well, really," he said, "is this absolutely essential?" John and Henry stopped fighting abruptly and climbed sheepishly to their feet. Henry's nose was bleeding; he felt hastily for a handkerchief. "It sounded," said the Major, "like an earthquake from downstairs."

"I'm sorry, sir," muttered John, looking at his feet.

"That handkerchief is no use, Henry," said Major Holbrooke, "go and hang over a basin. The rest of you had better tidy up and go to bed, then perhaps you'll feel in more agreeable frames of mind to-morrow. Good night," he added as he left the room.

"Lawks," said Christopher.

"Cheer up, John," said Noel, picking up a chair; "he didn't seem very cross about it."

"He's probably furious," said John, "but he doesn't show it. He'll never ask me to stay again," he added, thinking of another occasion when the Major had found him giving vent to his unlucky temper.

"Well, for that matter he won't ask me again either," said Christopher, "to-night at dinner was the third time I've upset the salt."

"I should think he'll give up the Pony Club altogether when we've lost his bet with Colonel Shellbourne for him," said Noel.

"We shan't do that, shall we?" asked Christopher. "I mean we've only got to be better than we were before and that's not difficult."

"Well, Merry, June and Henry don't try at all," said John indignantly, "they're simply out to sabotage the whole show."

"And Colonel Shellbourne isn't very noticing," said Noel. "We shall have had to improve quite a lot for him to see it. He won't admire our correct leg positions because he doesn't believe in them, but only the results of our having adopted them."

"Well, I'm going to bed," said John, picking up the last of the bagatelle balls, "I've got a filthy headache."

"Would you like an aspirin?" asked Noel. "There are some in the bathroom."

"What was going on?" asked Mrs. Holbrooke when the Major returned to the library.

"Henry and John were fighting," he answered.

"Did you tick them off?" asked Mrs. Holbrooke.

"No," answered the Major, "it's always impossible on these occasions to discover who was right or wrong. I told them to tidy up and go to bed."

"Of course John always has been quick tempered," said Mrs. Holbrooke.

"Yes, but Henry can be very irritating," said the Major. "I've often felt like hitting him myself. I expect there were faults on both sides. As Nanny used to say to the boys, 'It takes two to make a quarrel.' Anyway John's riding has improved a lot these holidays, he's really beginning to take an interest, I think. I'm going to let him ride the Merry Widow to-morrow, I want him to get the feel of a collected horse; one can talk and talk and talk, but they don't really understand what one means until they've ridden a horse which knows all about it."

"Well, you'd better think of an amusement for them in the evenings," said Mrs. Holbrooke, "or they'll be fighting again. What about a nice game of hide and seek or murder? You used to be rather good at playing when the boys were young."

"Thank you," said the Major, rather indignantly. "But my playing days are over and anyway I have the wretched children all morning and most of the afternoon. I think it's your duty to amuse them in the evening; you could show them round the aviary and finish up with a nice game of draughts."

CHAPTER FIVE

John was overjoyed when the Major told him at breakfast that he was to ride the Merry Widow. He was pleased partly because it is always interesting to ride a strange horse, particularly if it is well-bred and highly schooled, partly because it was a compliment to be allowed to ride the Major's horses, but chiefly because it was obvious that he wasn't in disgrace for fighting Henry. However, John wasn't one of those people who show their feelings, so he said, "Oh, thank you," and relapsed into his usual silence.

There was a good deal of excitement among the other Pony Club members when they heard about the fight. Merry said that it was obviously that odious boy John's fault and that she definitely couldn't stand him. June exclaimed, "Fancy two great boys like that fighting. Whatever did the Major think?" Roger said that he didn't think that it mattered so much what the Major had thought as what he had said and, when Christopher had told them the actual words he had used all over again, Dick said that he did hope John and Henry would stop being such idiots. Hilary said that she didn't see anything in a perfectly ordinary fight to get excited about and she thought that they were making a mountain out of a molehill. Roger told her that she had a bovine temperament and she answered that anything was better than being hysterical.

John realised that they were all talking about him and this combined with his swollen lip to make him feel very silly and self-conscious; he wished very much that he had kept his temper with Henry, who carried the whole thing off with a gay "don't care" air. But at last the news that

John was riding the Merry Widow changed the topic of conversation. Merry and June agreed, once again, that the Major was mad. Who, in their senses, would let such a heavy-handed lump ride a blood horse? Merry said that she wouldn't have him on Quaver for a hundred pounds.

John, feeling very high up and conspicuous in the lead, did not come in for much correction, except for being told to lighten his hands by opening his fingers a little. It was Merry, Christopher and Noel who were criticised the most. None of them were using their seats or legs enough; Sonnet looked like something out of a milk float and Merry's legs were still too far forward. Then the Major asked for an extended trot and everyone rode round the school at his fastest trot and was horrified to hear the Major exclaim that he couldn't tell it from the ordinary pace. "Come into the centre, everyone," he called. "I can't bear to see that horrible sight again. Henry, can I have Black Magic please. I think I'd better demonstrate." Henry dismounted and handed his horse over. "First," said the Major, "the collected trot; you merely use your seat, the horse becomes full of energy, which you restrain, very gently, with your hands." He rode off round the school. "Notice," he said, "how well-balanced she is, how her hocks are right under her, and the short appearance of her body. Now I'm going to trot on extendedly. Very gradually I push her on with my legs, giving at the same time with my hands, but I never lose contact with her mouth. Notice that she is still balanced, that I am using my legs and hands to keep her so and she is covering the ground with long, free strides. Can you tell the difference?" he asked as he pulled up.

"Yes, easily," answered all the members at once.

"She looks quite different from what she does when you're riding her, Henry," said Christopher.

"Twice the horse," agreed Roger Radcliffe.

"Now when you're trying to ride a shortened trot none

of you use your seat bones—I know you think you do, but you don't——" said the Major, "and when it comes to an extended trot you all sigh with relief; you think, thank goodness, no more cellection. You throw away your reins and you turtle round the school flapping your legs occasionally, all quite convinced that it is an extended trot. But it isn't even trotting; your horse can't trot properly with all their weight on their forehands; they can't stride out; it's simply a horrible unbalanced run. Now come on, try again and let's see if you can't do it a bit better. And remember to change your diagonals, now that you're going round the opposite way; it doesn't matter which you're on as long as you change it each time you change the rein."

All the members were exhausted when it came to passes, so Major Holbrooke said that he would give them five minutes' rest. Everyone dismounted, loosened their horse's girth and took off any of their own clothes which weren't absolutely essential; then they sat on the grass holding their horses until the five minutes were up. The Major's first question, "Who knows the aids?" caused a good deal of despondency. Susan found that she had forgotten them; Henry had never known them. June said that she knew them like the palm of her hand, but she couldn't put them into so many words. The Radcliffes said that you did this and this and demonstrated with their arms and legs, but the Major told them that they looked like windmills and that he wanted to have the aids explained properly. John and Dick knew that you used the diagonal aids; that to half pass from right to left you would feel your left rein and press with your right leg just behind the girth. They knew that you brought your right hand a little to the left and used your left leg on the girth to keep your horse up to his bit. But only Noel knew that the horse's head should be bent slightly in the direction of the movement, and that the rider must look in the direction he wished to go, and the

Major had to drag that out of her. When they got down to riding, the despondency grew, for no one seemed to pass correctly, though most of the members had practised before.

Noel's chief fault was that she would look down at the ground and Sonnet lacked impulsion. June was soon in trouble because her hands were in her stomach again and, when Golden Glory napped towards the other horses, she was too late in using her legs. The Merry Widow and Black Magic were both very good at passes, but the Major had to tell John, "More right leg and less left rein; you're pulling her round instead of pushing her over," and to Henry he said, "Put your right knee in, that's a very common fault. Now feel your left rein a little more. Can you see Magic's left eye? You should just be able to."

Crispin was inclined to lead with his quarters, which, the Major said, could be avoided by giving the rein aid a fraction of a second before the leg. When Dick tried this Crispin passed very well. Northwind, like Sonnet, lacked impulsion and he was also inclined to look in the wrong direction. Susan's first attempt was hopeless because she failed to go sideways at all, but her second try was quite good. Roger would persist in looking and leaning to the right, which meant that his legs and reins were telling Sky Pilot to go one way while his weight told him to go another. Merry, who had been making scornful and impatient noises during everyone else's turn, decided to do a little showing off. She had read somewhere that the full pass was more difficult than the half pass, so she attempted to full pass across the school. "Legs," shouted the Major; "that horse is behind the bit, send him forward."

"Oh, but I thought you wanted a full pass," said Merry, feeling rather disappointed.

"You can't have been attending," said the Major disagreeably, "or you would have seen what the others were doing."

"It was impossible," muttered Merry, "to tell what they were *supposed* to be doing."

"What's that?" asked the Major sharply.

But Merry thought better of her remark for she only said "Nothing," and pouted.

Christopher's turn came last, which was just as well, as Fireworks wasn't feeling obliging. He was willing to pass from left to right, but he seemed to think that to do so in the opposite direction was impossible.

"Bring him up to the hedge," said the Major, when all his other advice had failed, "halt him facing it. Now apply the aids and just try to get a few steps in the right direction. Harder with your leg," he went on as Fireworks persisted in going in the wrong direction. "Try again, and if he goes against your leg, back it up with your stick."

Fireworks did go against his leg, so Christopher used his stick and then the pony decided that the time had come to be obliging and hastily passed in the right direction. "Pat him," said the Major. "Now walk him round the school, bring him up to the hedge and try again." This time Fireworks passed to the left without any fuss. Then Major Holbrooke told everyone to walk on round the school holding their reins only at the buckle and allowing their horses to stretch out their necks. This, he said, was called the free walk. And it was very important to remember to ride your horse round the school a couple of times at the free walk after each five or ten minutes of collected work.

"By the way, Noel," he went on, "you're not meant to relax too. You drop the reins, but you still use your legs. Make your pony walk out; from the moment you mount until the moment you dismount you should never allow her to dawdle."

"Sorry," said Noel, blushing slightly and applying her legs with vigour.

Later they jumped. Christopher was sent away to a far

corner of the field to continue Fireworks' schooling over a very low fence. The others also began with a low jump and the Major corrected their positions. When they were all jumping reasonably well, they crossed their stirrups and jumped without and afterwards they knotted their reins as well, and jumped, folding their arms as their horses took off and picking up the reins when they had landed. Merry didn't think much of jumping like this; she told June that such circus tricks were all very well if you had a suitable horse, but that Quaver was much too hot for that sort of thing.

June said that Glory hadn't been able to make it out at first but that now she was doing quite well considering that she was a thoroughbred. Merry replied that some half-breds were even hotter than thoroughbreds—it was a matter of temperament.

"They're not as difficult to ride as thoroughbreds," said June.

"Rubbish," replied Merry, "it depends entirely on the horse. Look at Quaver, he's as hot as any race horse, much hotter than Glory."

"He charges about more," said June, "but that's just bad manners. He must be an uncomfortable ride."

"He's nothing of the sort," said Merry furiously. "He's hot and he's tireless and he takes hold a bit, but I'd rather have that than a nappy animal always behind the bit."

"How much longer have we got to wait for you two to stop gossiping?" inquired the Major wearily.

"Oh, what are we supposed to do?" asked Merry.

"If you had been attending you would know," said the Major sternly. "As you jump the small fence in front of you, you endeavour to take the handkerchief from the post."

What a mad idea, thought Merry as she rode at the jump; anyone could do this. But, as she bent to grab the handkerchief, Quaver twisted and jumped sideways, away from the post, and off fell Merry. She got to her feet quite quickly, but, finding that her back hurt a little, she put on an agonised face and hobbled slowly across to where John was holding Quaver. She didn't thank John; she just said, "*Can't* you keep him still?" peevishly, as she tried to mount.

The other members were jumping, but so far no one had succeeded in grabbing the handkerchief. John had another try but, he too, failed.

"It's impossible, Uncle," grumbled Henry, "this horse is too tall."

"You are a hopeless crew," said the Major. "Well, if Merry doesn't want another try, I'll show you how it is done. Can I have Black Magic?"

"With pleasure," said Henry. To everyone's annoyance the Major managed to pick up the handkerchief at his first attempt. "It's only a matter of placing your horse," he told them. "Make him jump close to the post and it's easy, but of course you must use your legs."

"Can we have another try?" asked Henry.

"Of course," he answered, replacing the handkerchief.

"I do wish I could have a go," said Christopher, who sat watching on Fireworks.

"Here, have Wonder," said Susan, jumping off.

"Oh, thanks awfully," said Christopher. "You're sure it's all right?"

"Of course," answered Susan. "I should think you'd have the stirrups up two."

In the end everyone but Merry managed to pick up the handkerchief. She stood about looking very sorry for herself and, when anyone asked what was the matter with her, she answered, "Nothing, it's only my back."

Except for the fact that Merry never turned up and the

Major gave a lecture on flexion, Thursday was a very uneventful day. Some people—the Radcliffes for instance—found the lecture dull, but they managed to keep up an appearance of interest to avoid yawning.

The Major explained the action of the double bridle on the horse's mouth and the response which they wished him to make to it, direct flexion. "When horses are balanced, going well, full of impulsion with their heads carried high and their hocks under them we may ask them to collect; in other words to bend at the poll and flex their lower jaw, so that we may have all that impulsion we have created controlled by the lightest touch of our little fingers. As you all know, the action of the snaffle is to raise the horse's head; to collect him you use your curb bit in conjunction with a properly adjusted curb chain. Now I'll demonstrate with Wonder. I feel the curb rein, the bit presses on the bars of the mouth, the curb chain in the chin groove; the horse is uncomfortable, but, as soon as he relaxes his lower jaw, thus giving to the bit or flexing, the pressure will cease and he will be comfortable, *provided* that the rider keeps his hands still. You see that as soon as Wonder flexes the reins become almost loose; I have only the very lightest contact with her mouth. There is a danger that people who have not cultivated light hands will not feel this contact and will move their hands or shorten their reins in order to establish a firmer feel of their horse's mouth. It is extremely important that you shouldn't do this for, as you will realise, the horse, having obeyed the bit and relaxed his jaw, expects his reward in the shape of comfort, which he will automatically obtain if your hands remain still."

At the end of the lesson he apologised for its dullness. "I'm afraid that it's all been walking and talking this morning," he said, "but the most important things always seem to be dull in the beginning. However, to-morrow I've unfortunately to go to London on business, so you will be able to relax—it will do the horses good to have a day off from schooling, we don't want them to become stale—you can go for a hack and on Saturday we shall break new ground, which, I think, you will find interesting."

"I think it's all interesting," said Dick.

"So do I," agreed Noel, who had been wishing to say so for some time, but lacked the courage.

"Hear, hear," said John. The other members murmured in agreement.

"Thank you," said the Major. "And now, has anyone any questions?"

"Yes," said Christopher promptly. "Shall I be able to ride Fireworks in the hunter trials? I mean will he jump well enough by then?"

"He jumps well enough now," answered the Major. "He's got tremendous spring, plenty of scope and courage and good sound legs, all he lacks is manners and he's improving quite quickly. I think he will be able to enter."

"Oh, hurray," said Christopher.

"Go on, Noel," said Susan. Noel blushed and said, "Ssh."

"But you must ask it," said Susan. "I want to know the answer too."

"Well, ask it then," muttered Noel; "it's a silly question."

"Uncle George, there's another question coming," said Henry. "Only Noel's gone bashful."

"Oh you are beastly," said Noel. "It was only that you talked about a properly adjusted curb chain," she said to Major Holbrooke, "and I've never been able to discover how you tell when a curb chain is properly adjusted. All the books I've read say 'The curb chain must neither be too tight nor too loose,' which isn't awfully helpful." And she sat looking at her reins and thinking that there was probably some fearfully obvious way of telling, which she had been told dozens of times and just forgotten.

"That's a very sensible question," said the Major. "First of all, as you all know, the curb chain must be twisted flat; when it is hooked on, the top side should be a little farther from the chin grooves than the lower side. Having checked those two points, pull the curb reins gently and watch the bit cheeks and the curb chain. When the reins are slack the bit cheeks lie along the horse's lips, and when you pull the reins the cheeks move away: when there is an angle of forty-five degrees between the bit cheek and the lips the curb chain should come into contact with the horse's chin groove. Forty-five degrees is half a right angle. For a young horse or an indifferent rider, who were not used to a double bridle, we would adjust the curb chain a couple of links looser, but we must remember that the action of the curb is lost if the curb chain is too loose. If the curb chain is too tight the action of the bit will be too sudden and too severe and the horse, becoming frightened of his mouth, will go behind the bit. And now," he added, "it's time for lunch."

CHAPTER SIX

MAJOR and Mrs. Holbrooke, having told the Pony Club members not to quarrel or do anything silly, caught an early train to London. When they had gone Henry, John, Noel and Christopher wandered down to the stables and began to groom their mounts. Soon Roger and Hilary arrived with the news that Evelyn, Margaret and James were riding over and bringing their lunch. "Oh goody," said Susan, who had arrived a moment later, "we shall have some fun now; Evelyn's awfully good at thinking of things to do."

"Oh goody," said Henry, imitating her voice, "what sort of things—dollies' tea parties?"

"Oh, Henry, how can you?" said Susan, laughing. "You know what sort of things I mean, races and games on horses."

"But I didn't know," objected Henry. "After all, I've never met Evelyn."

"Well, you're going to in a moment," said Roger. "I hear hoofs."

"Oh goody," exclaimed Henry.

The last person to arrive was June. "I didn't tell Mummy that the Major was away," she explained when the empty trailer had disappeared down the drive, "because she wouldn't have let me come."

"Why ever not?" asked Hilary.

"Oh I don't know," answered June carelessly, "she's terribly fussy about what I do with Glory."

"No sign of Merry," said Noel, who had ridden down the drive to see if she was coming.

"She's much too seriously injured to ride," said Hilary sarcastically. "She's probably visiting all the orthopaedic surgeons in Harley Street."

"One's never quite sure," said Dick. "One makes up one's mind that a person isn't hurt, and then afterwards it turns out that they were and one is haunted by remorse."

"I don't see why," said John, "after all it's only a perfectly ordinary mistake and one can't help making them sometimes."

"You've no imagination," Henry told him, "so of course you don't understand."

"Henry, I'll tell your uncle of you," shouted Christopher. "You know he forbade all quarrelling."

"I wasn't quarrelling," said Henry crossly. "I was making an interesting statement."

"No interesting statements allowed if relating to persons present," said Dick. "Everyone may criticise Merry as much as they like."

"Come on, let's ride," said Evelyn.

"We thought we might use the big flat field by the Hogshill road," said Roger to Henry, "do you think it'll be O.K.?"

"Sure," said Henry.

The field was about ten acres in size; perfectly flat and level, it was a super place for races.

"What shall we do first?" asked Susan.

"Have a gallop round," said Evelyn at once and she galloped off as fast as Northwind—Hilary was riding Rocket to-day—could be persuaded to go.

"Yoicks, tally-ho!" yelled Roger, tearing after her and passing her in a few moments. Henry gave a view holloa and followed flat out on Black Magic, who was very fast indeed. The other Pony Club members followed, but at a more leisurely pace, except for Fireworks; he gave three bucks and tore after the leaders.

They galloped round the field twice and then everyone pulled up, except Fireworks, but, after tugging him round in a couple of circles Christopher managed to stop too.

"That was *super*," said John.

"Terrific, fantastic, etc.," said Christopher, who seemed rather out of breath.

"Sonnet's miles faster than I thought," said Noel. "It must be the Major's oats."

"Yes, she's just as fast as Wonder," said Susan.

"What next?" asked Henry.

"A walk, trot and canter race?" suggested Hilary.

"Yes," said the other Radcliffes. They explained to the people who didn't know that circling was the penalty for trotting at the walking or cantering at the trotting stage and then they agreed that James should start the race because he was the youngest.

"I think I ought to have a start," said Margaret.

"Oh, no, at least your pony's used to it," said June. "Glory's never done anything of this sort before."

Fireworks began to race at a gallop, though he was supposed to be walking. Golden Wonder bucked, star-gazed and refused to go straight. Golden Glory jogged and cantered on the spot. Henry won the race, Evelyn was second and John third. "Next time the little ponies must have a start," grumbled Margaret.

"Now a relay race," said Evelyn. "Who's going to pick?"

"The eldest, to avoid argument," suggested Dick. "Wake up, Noel," shouted Evelyn. "Henry's picked you."

"Oh," said Noel. "Whatever for?"

"To tell me who to pick next," said Henry when she joined him.

"John, Dick and Susan," answered Noel. "The Radcliffes always like to pick each other."

"I draw the line at the man in the street," said Henry, picking Dick.

"Oh, Henry, you are a fool," said Christopher when he was picked before John.

The Radcliffes and John won easily. Christopher became hopelessly out of control and galloped twice round the field and Noel dropped the riding stick she was trying to hand to June.

"Now a touch-the-corners race," said Margaret. "I'll go against Noel or Susan."

"Don't organise, Marga," said Hilary.

"Something has occurred to me," said Henry, "surely my esteemed Uncle George told us to go for a hack?"

"Oh golly, so he did," exclaimed Susan.

"I think he only meant the horses were to have a rest from schooling, didn't he?" asked Roger.

"I expect he was afraid that they were becoming constricted," said Evelyn. "It's a well-known fact that too much schooling ruins any horse, but you couldn't have anything much better for a constricted animal than this."

"It doesn't seem to have improved Fireworks," said Dick.

"Shall we go for a quiet hack now?" suggested Noel. "I think Fireworks needs calming down."

"Taking him for a silly little hack won't calm him down," said Evelyn. "You want to let him gallop, Christopher, he'll tire himself out in the end."

"What a hope," said Christopher.

"Advice from the expert," said Henry, "but I'm going for a hack. I think we've had quite enough races."

"I'll come too, if that's O.K.," said Noel.

"A pleasure," said Henry, with a bow. "Any more?"

"Me," said Susan.

"No fear," said John, who really thought that Henry

was quite right, but had no intention of admitting it. You're not going, are you, Dick?"

"Well, I must say I think Henry's right."

"Oh, you're all Holbrooke-ridden," said Evelyn impatiently. "You're going to become the sort of people who never let their horses out of a collected canter even when hounds are running. Don't go with that feeble lot," she added aside to Dick.

"All right," said Dick, rather against his will.

"You go with them, Jim," said Hilary quietly. "We know you don't like races."

"If you don't think it's feeble?" said James, who suffered from being the least tough member of the family.

"No, go on, don't take any notice of Evelyn," said Hilary, who was more tolerant than her twin.

"I'm staying," said June, "I get plenty of hacking at home and I hate it."

"Good for you, June," said Evelyn.

"Come on, girls," said Henry in Evelyn's voice. "Three cheers for June, the heroine of St. Crispin's." He added, "Shall we jump the hedge on the way out?"

"Yes," answered Noel, "you give us a lead."

"You'd better go through the gate, Jim," said Susan. "The hedge looks a bit high for Darkie."

Black Magic cleared the hedge easily, Golden Wonder and Sonnet followed without hesitation, but Sonnet brushed through it with her hind legs.

Henry pulled up and waited for James. "Now where shall we go?" he asked.

"Across the fields to the Roman road?" suggested Noel and the others agreed. First a grassy track led through the cornfields; it was very hot under the blazing sun and the corn seemed to be ripening before their eyes. Then they skirted a beechwood, a cool, green oasis in the midst of the burning wold, and came to a barley field, cut and baled.

They cantered on till they reached a strip of uncultivated land, scattered with stunted thorns and undermined with rabbit warrens, among which they had to pick their way carefully. One more cornfield separated them from the Roman road; there was no path to follow so they rode single file round the headland and climbed the steep bank to the road which, here, was raised above the fields. They stood in a row looking across the simmering downland, noticing here and there a tiny village tucked away in the folds of the hills, a grey, square church or a toy-like farm, and in the distant valley the silver river winding.

It was wonderful, thought Henry, to stand there with a tiny breeze blowing in your face and watch the panorama of the countryside unfold itself at your feet. The world seemed incredibly lovely. He sighed. Why weren't all days like this one? Why did it have to rain and snow? Why did one have to be bad tempered and cold and liverish? Why did one have to grow up and work in offices? Noel felt the same pleasure as the breeze stirred her dark hair and she knew the same joy as she gazed across the fields, but James thought that nothing inland could beat the majesty of the sea and Susan wondered why some people got so excited over views. "The others were idiots not to come," said Henry, breaking the silence. "This is much better than a touch-the-corners race or whatever it was called."

" 'I strove with none, for none were worth my strife'," said Noel dreamily.

" 'Nature I loved and next to Nature art'," continued Henry as he turned and led the way along the Roman road.

"For goodness' sake don't encourage Noel," said Susan. "You don't know what she's like once she starts spouting; she can keep it up for hours."

"The only poem I know all through is the 'Fighting Temeraire'," said James, "but when I've time, I'm going to learn 'Drake's Drum'."

"I should learn the 'Ancient Mariner', it's got some nice creepy bits," said Noel.

"The others *were* idiots, weren't they?" said Henry a little later.

"Complete idiots," agreed Noel.

"It was the Radcliffes' influence," said Henry in a low voice. "I detest your friend Evelyn," he added to Susan.

"Ssh," said Noel, "James will hear."

"No, he won't," replied Henry, "he's too far behind, and anyway he's thinking about the 'Fighting Temeraire'. But surely you can't like Evelyn? She's just as frightful as Merry."

"But we all thought you liked Merry," said Susan in a surprised voice. "John said that you were the perfect couple and ought to marry."

"John allowed his personal animosity to blind his judgment," said Henry firmly. "Anyway if I've got to marry Merry you can marry John and I bet he leads you a life; he'll always be disagreeable at breakfast."

"Oh, Henry, you are silly," said Susan with a giggle.

"Oh am I? Really? Goody, goody," said Henry, imitating her voice.

Down below in the valley the touch-the-corners race had been won by Evelyn and had been followed, in turn, by an obstacle, a leaf collecting and a trotting race. A Gretna Green race had been arranged, after a great deal of arguing about who should go with whom, and won by Dick and Evelyn. Fireworks had refused to stop at all and John, who had been Christopher's partner, had given the race up as a bad job.

"I think that we might stop now," said Dick when the Gretna Green was over. "It's fearfully hot and I wouldn't mind jumping a couple of hedges on the way back to the stables."

"Good idea," said John.

"Oh, we can't stop yet," said Evelyn. "It's only twelve o'clock. Be a sport, Dick; we must have one more race."

"Oh yes, we *must*," echoed Margaret, "we've hardly had any."

"Well, I'll stay for one more," said Dick, "but only one."

"All right, so will I," said John.

"Why don't you gallop Fireworks round the field a few times?" suggested Evelyn to Christopher. "He's still as fresh as ever."

"It'll only make him worse," answered Christopher. "I ought to have taken him for a hack really."

"He's terribly hot," said June. "Look how lathered he is; I should walk him about."

"No fear," replied Christopher, "anything to stand still and give my arms a rest, they've been pulled almost out of their sockets."

"I'll tell you what—a saddling-up race," said Evelyn suddenly.

"Oh yes, beginning bareback," said Roger. "Leave the saddles here and we'll start from the other end of the field."

The saddles were arranged in a row along the fence. June asked Roger to give her a leg up, Christopher climbed on Fireworks from the gate, the others could all vault on their mounts. Margaret was the starter because she was the youngest. In the first wild gallop across the field Glory bucked and June rolled off, but she jumped to her feet and pursued Glory, who trotted to the gate, Margaret had her saddle on first; visions of beating her brother and sisters as well as John and Dick spurred her on. She scrambled up; Pixie stood like a rock, but the saddle slipped a little. She looked round; John and Evelyn were both mounting. "Come on, Pixie," shrieked Margaret, and, waving her arms and legs like windmills, she urged her pony forward.

As Pixie began to canter the saddle began to slip; it slipped and slipped until suddenly Margaret found herself on the ground gazing up at the patient Pixie, who stood with the saddle upside down under her tummy.

"Are you all right?" shouted Hilary, galloping past.

"Yes," shrieked Margaret, leaping to her feet. If she hurried she wouldn't be last; June and Christopher were still behind her. June was mounting, but Fireworks wouldn't stand still. Christopher got his foot in the stirrups and jumped for it, but before he could swing his leg over, Fireworks was off at a gallop. Christopher tried to pull him up and tried to get on, but he couldn't do either so he just hung on for grim death; they galloped past Glory. "Whoa, whoa," shouted June when she saw what had happened. The others members turned. "Crikey!" said John. "Whoa, Fireworks; whoa, boy," called Hilary. "Hang on, Christopher," shouted Dick. "Perhaps he'll stop when he gets here," said Roger. But Fireworks didn't stop; he swerved and galloped towards the hedge. The Pony Club members stood feeling very helpless. "Can't we corner him?" suggested Evelyn. John's heart seemed to be in the wrong place. Then Fireworks swerved again and Christopher lost his hold of the saddle and fell; for a horrid moment he was mixed up with Fireworks' flying hoofs and then the pony galloped on and he lay there alone. The Pony Club members waited for a moment hoping to see him leap to his feet, but he didn't and with sinking hearts they cantered across the field. As they reached him he got up. He looked dazed.

"I'm . . . I'm all right," he said. "What happened?"

"Fireworks went off at a gallop with you half on," John told him.

"You were jolly good to stick on as long as you did!" said Evelyn.

"Where am I?" asked Christopher.

"At Folly Court," said John.

"What's happened?" asked Christopher.

The Pony Club members looked at each other in dismay.

"He's concussed," said Roger. "He ought to have been wearing a hat," said Hilary.

"We *have* done it now," said John.

"Where am I? What's happened? Why won't you tell me?" demanded Christopher angrily.

"Oh dear, I'm sure he's gone mad," said Margaret, miserably.

"Don't be silly," said Roger, who intended to follow in his father's footsteps and become a doctor. "We must put him to bed in a darkened room. Complete quiet is essential."

"What's happened? Oh, why won't you tell me?" asked Christopher tearfully. John hastily told him all over again.

"We had better take him up to the house," said Dick. "If someone will take Crispin, I'll walk with him."

"I'd better come with you," said John, "because I know my way about."

"Right, we'll put the horses away," said Roger.

"I'll catch Fireworks," said Hilary. It was a mournful procession which wended its way up the long back drive to the stables. Five riders, three of them leading riderless horses and behind John and Dick, walking one on either side of Christopher and answering, again and again, those same questions. "Where am I? What's happened? What day is it? What happened?" Dick soon began to feel that he would scream if it went on much longer and he marvelled at John's patience as he went on and on answering in the same even tone of voice. "It's quite all right, Christoper; you're at Folly Court."

"I did this once at rugger," John told Dick in a rare moment of silence.

"If only he had his crash cap on," said Dick.

"Yes, we were fools to take them off," said John.

"I hope he'll be better by the time the Holbrookes come home," said Dick, "it's going to be a bit awkward otherwise; the Major did tell us to go for a hack."

"Still Christopher might easily have fallen off out for a ride," said John.

They took off Christopher's jodhs and shoes and shoved him into bed. John drew the curtains and then they hurried out before he could begin to ask "Where am I?" again.

The hacking party had returned and were being told the sad tale by the time that John and Dick reached the stable yard. Henry said, "Oh Lord," and "Blast everything; it would happen when Uncle George was out." Noel, wishing that she had withstood the Radcliffe influence and made Christopher go for a hack, asked, "Should we send for a doctor?"

Susan could only exclaim, "Oh golly!" and "How awful." But Blake said that he should wait till after lunch and if the boy wasn't better then, he should send for the doctor; it was always best to be on the safe side. The Radcliffes looked rather miserable at this and Roger explained, when Blake had gone, that as their father was both the Minton's and the Holbrooke's doctor they would have to send for him *and* tell him what had happened. "And that," he finished, "would mean two lectures instead of one."

At this point the gong rang for the Folly Court lunch, so Henry, John and Noel left the others to their sandwiches and dashed indoors. They explained Christopher's accident to Hilda, the cook, who had worked for the Holbrookes for years. She told Henry that he had better fetch Nanny—who had brought up all the Holbrooke boys and now lived at the Lodge—for she was quite used to dealing with people who had fallen off. Henry said, "Of course; why on earth didn't I think of it before? I'll run down to the Lodge now." He tore off down the drive and the others waited rather gloomily for his return. He was soon back and told them that she would be along in about ten minutes.

They sat down to lunch with lighter hearts now that an expert was coming on the scene. When the expert arrived, Henry conducted her to Christopher's room, but he was asleep and Nanny said that he mustn't be disturbed.

"You go and clean your harness," she told them in a voice that was used to command. "I'll stay and see how he is when he wakens."

"Oh, Nanny, you're marvellous," said Henry in flattering accents.

Merry was in the saddle room talking to the other members. She was wearing a fashionable summer dress and high-heeled shoes.

"I'm simply furious," said Merry to Henry. "I've come for my grooming tools and tack cleaning things and they're all lost, all muddled up among other peoples. I think it's simply *disgraceful*; why can't people keep their hands off my property? I shall write to Major Holbrooke. I think it's the absolute limit."

"Oh, my poor dear, how too fraightful for you," said Henry in a languid and affected voice. "But why are you trying to find all these sets of tools; are you giving up dressage?"

"Yes," answered Merry, "the specialist says that I'm not to ride for at least a week."

"Cheers," muttered John.

"Have you told me esteemed Uncle G.?" asked Henry.

"I've brought a note for him," answered Merry.

"What exactly is the matter with your back?" asked Roger.

"I had it X-rayed yesterday," Merry told them impressively.

"And what did they find?" asked Roger.

"No bonal injury," answered Merry shortly.

"It can't be much then," said Evelyn.

"Oh can't it?" said Merry indignantly. "My back's severely sprained; it's agony at times, I can tell you."

"Very painful I should think," said June, trying to look wise. "I remember once I sprained my wrist——"

"Look, I must have my tools," interrupted Merry. "Who's had them?"

"How should we know?" asked Roger.

"I bet Christopher's hidden them," said Merry furiously.

"Oh no, he hasn't," said John, "he's not a bit interested in your beastly property."

"Hadn't we better clean our tack?" said Dick.

"Oh golly, yes," said Susan. "I was told not to be late for tea—we've got visitors and that means changing."

"You're always having visitors," said Noel.

"Yes, and they're all terribly dull, they only talk about shops and cooking—it's awful," said Susan.

"It's going to be awful here to-night," said John.

"Why?" asked June.

"Explaining to the Holbrookes, of course," answered John. "All you lucky devils will have gone home and I shall be the only person who was actually there when Christopher came off."

"We'll support you, John," said Noel.

"I think you're making a fuss about nothing," said Evelyn. "After all people must fall off occasionally and the Holbrookes aren't nervous old ladies. Christopher took a perfectly ordinary toss—it was just bad luck that he hurt himself."

"The whole point," said Henry, "is that it wasn't a perfectly ordinary toss. Uncle George would be the last person to fuss if it were. We were supposed to be hacking and we all know that Fireworks is a menace."

"And that we're supposed to wear hard hats," said Noel.

"Well, you needn't go in to all that," said Evelyn.

"You've no morals," Henry told her, "but anyway it's obvious from a mile off that we've got guilty consciences. Look at John's hangdog appearance."

"I think I'd better stay and support you," said Dick. "After all, I was there."

"I wouldn't bother, Dick," said Henry. "Uncle G. won't eat us, you know; at the worst he'll curse and swear a bit."

"I've finished my tack," said John. "I'll go and see how Christopher is."

"Oh, John," exclaimed June in shocked accents. "You can't have done it properly."

When all the other Pony Club members had gone home, Noel and Henry found John, who said that Christopher was still asleep and tea was on the lawn near the aviary.

"You'll have to pour out," Henry told Noel as they sat down. It was a lovely evening and they sat for some time after they had finished tea, basking in the warmth of the slanting sun, watching the shadows of the trees lengthen across the lawn, listening to the solos of the wild birds and the chorus from the aviary. "Have you ever seen round the aviary?" asked Henry, breaking a long silence.

"No, but I've always wanted to," answered Noel.

"If you like I'll take you round when we've turned out the horses," offered Henry, "provided, of course, that my relations haven't returned."

"That would be lovely," said Noel.

"Super," agreed John.

They turned out the horses and gave the barn its final sweeping up—the Pony Club members who came each day always did their stable work at lunch-time—and then, when they returned to the house, they were met by Nanny, who said that Christopher was awake and quite sensible, but that he was bothering about what had happened and whether his pony was all right. "You'd better go and tell 'im," said Nanny, "but don't stay long and don't make a noise."

Christopher sat up and grinned when they appeared.

"How are you feeling?" asked Noel.

"I've only got a bit of a headache," he answered, "but you might tell me what happened. I can't remember a thing." They told him about the unsaddling race, how he had come off, and what he had said and then they told him that they had better go or Nanny would be after them.

"Thank heavens he's all right," said Henry as they ran downstairs, "and now for a look round the aviary. Mind you, I don't know what half of the wretched birds are," he added as he opened the door.

Noel said, "This is certainly a lovely place for them, though I don't really agree with keeping birds in aviaries."

"But they're not wild birds," explained Henry, "they were born in captivity; they don't know what to do if you let them out."

"Now," he went on, adopting a guide book manner, "this brightly coloured little bird is a native of South Africa. Aunt Carol has endeavoured to reproduce his native haunts, not that he ever saw them—by this mass of pampas grass, among which, his less colourful mate is lurking—pass along to the next cage, please. Here we have the budgerigars or grass parakeets, natives, I believe, of Australia. Beyond them you recognise, of course, the common canary, but you may not be aware that in his wild state—in the Canary Islands—his plumage is green. There's a pair of green ones next door. The next few cages are all different sorts of pigeons and this is Achibald, he's a cockatoo."

"He looks like a parrot," said John.

"Well, he isn't," said Henry, "he's a cockatoo, they come from Malaya."

"He's very handsome," said Noel, looking at his pink and white plumage and parroty beak.

"He's a cunning old devil," said Henry, "aren't you, Archie?"

"No, no, no," replied Archibald promptly.

"Don't tell lies," said Henry.

"No, no, no," screamed Archie indignantly. "Take me out, take me out," he asked, putting his head on one side and looking at them with his little beady eyes.

"Is he tame?" asked Noel.

"Oh yes," answered Henry, "he lives in a cage in the house all the winter and he's allowed out as long as there is someone about to see that he doesn't get eaten by cats or anything."

"Can you make him say anything else?" asked John.

"I'll try," said Henry. "Good old Archie; you are a pretty fellow; I'm very fond of you," said Henry in affectionate accents. Archie put his head even more on one side, and asked, in a sentimental voice, "Shall we kiss?"

"No fear," said John.

"No, no, no," shrieked Archie.

"My cousin Roland taught him that one," said Henry. "He used to persuade Archie to say it when David had girl friends to stay."

"You could have awfully good fun with him, I should think," said John. "Imagine having one at school."

"Take me out," said Archie.

"Aunt Carol used to have a proper parrot which would converse for hours," said Henry, "but, of course, Archie's only about eight so he's still plenty of time to learn."

"Take me out," said Archie.

"You're nearly as bad as Christopher," said John.

"Take me out; Oh yes," said Archie pleadingly.

"Well, I suppose we might let you out in the passageway while we look at the other birds, but you're to behave yourself and you're not going out in the garden, so you needn't think it," said Henry sternly.

"Oh, yes," answered Archie. Henry opened the cage, picked Archie up and put him on Noel's shoulder.

"You are lovely," Noel told Archie. "I think that you're terribly clever."

He seemed quite content to perch on her shoulder and she followed John and Henry to the next cage of birds. Suddenly, with a loud squawk, Archie flew down the passageway, he had noticed that the door was ajar; Noel—the last person in—had forgotten to shut it.

"Hell," said Henry as Archie flew out into the garden.

"Shall we ever catch him?" asked John aghast.

"Oh I am an idiot; why on earth didn't I shut the door?" said Noel miserably.

"Archie," called Henry, "come on, Archie, there's a good bird." But Archie merely answered, "No, no, no," and half flew, half hopped across the lawn. "If we could get him in the house we could corner him," said Henry, and with John and Noel on either side he tried to drive Archie towards the front door. But as soon as Archie realised what they were about he shrieked, "No, no, no," and flew round the corner of the house and down the path which led to the vegetable garden. Noel remembered with horror the last occasion on which she had pursued an escaped animal through the Holbrookes' garden. At least Archie didn't do so much damage as Topsy, thought Noel, as she recollected the state of the herbaceous border and the hoof-marks on the lawn. But it would be frightful if he were lost altogether.

"We might be able to catch him between the greenhouses," said Henry. "You go round the far side and lie in wait, John; we'll try to drive him down between them." John hurried on ahead, Henry and Noel shepherded Archie into a narrow path between short, fat box hedges and then drove him tactfully, in the direction of the greenhouses. He wandered along quite happily, stopping occasionally to peck at the path, but always keeping a wary eye on his pursuers. He entered the space between the greenhouses. "Look out, John," said Henry and John appeared, barring the way out of the trap.

"No, no, no," shrieked Archie, flying straight at John. "No, no, no," he squawked, dodging John's outstretched hands and flying over the corner of the greenhouse. John jumped and grabbed, but a handful of feathers were all that remained in his hand as he landed with a loud splintering of glass and a groan, which told Noel and Henry of further disaster.

"Oh, Lord, now what's he done?" said Henry.

"Oh blast everything," said John. "I've landed on a beastly cloche and smashed it to atoms."

"Well, thank heavens it wasn't the greenhouse," said Henry. "Where's that wretched bird gone now?"

"I've got half his feathers," said John.

"That will please Aunt Carol," said Henry sarcastically. "There he is," said Noel. "Look, in that apple-tree at the end of the garden." They ran across the garden, but by the time they reached the tree Archie had flown to a higher bough; none of them could reach him. "I'll climb up," said Henry. But each time Henry reached the bough where Archie was perching he flew to a higher one. At first Henry called to him in a kind voice, promising him biscuits, but he soon began to call him a maddening animal and threaten him with fearful deaths. At last, when he was at the top of the tree, he asked for a rake or hoe from the toolshed, for Archie was still perched out of reach, on a flimsy branch that would not bear Henry's weight. But, when Archie saw John handing the rake to Henry he gave a loud squawk and flew out of the tree across the garden and hopped through the thorn hedge to the drive. "Go on," shouted Henry to Noel and John. "Run . . . don't let him get out on the road." John and Noel rushed between the rows of lettuces, round the runner beans and over the box hedges; through the white iron gate to the drive. But Archie was ahead of them and each time they drew near he hopped or flew faster in the direction of the road. They climbed the rails into the park; John got ahead of him first and, climbing back into the drive, tried to stop Archie by waving his arms and saying shoo. But Archie dodged him again and flew even faster towards the road. Noel ran on, but when she reached the road Archie was nowhere to be seen.

Oh, dear, she thought, whatever do we do now? "There's not a sign of him," she said as John joined her. John said, "What a beastly day it is; everything is determined to go wrong."

"It was my fault," said Noel miserably.

Henry was cast into despair by their tidings. He said that it was dinner time; that his Aunt and Uncle must certainly be home and that no one would have the faintest idea where he, Noel and John were and heaven knew what sort of story they would be told about Christopher. John said, "Well, we'd better have a quick search before we go back and report the disaster."

And Noel said, "Look, there's someone coming up the road; perhaps she has seen him." As the passer-by drew near they could see that she wasn't a country person; she wore high-heeled shoes and a townish-looking hat. She was of middle age. "You ask her, Henry," said John.

Suddenly a familiar voice asked from the depths of a roadside bush, "Shall we kiss?" The passer-by stopped and looked about her suspiciously. Henry, John and Noel looked at each other and began to giggle; with one accord they drew back behind the hedge. "Shall we kiss?" repeated Archie in his most seductive tones. "Oh *yes.*" The woman blushed and walked on quickly. "No, no, no," shrieked Archie from the depths of his bush. The woman was almost running as she disappeared round a bend in the road.

"He *is* the limit," said Henry. "He quite upset that poor woman."

"She was fairly running down the road," said John.

"How *are* we going to catch him?" asked Noel, who was beginning to feel hungry.

"We'd better all go out in the road and drive him back," said Henry. "Come on, or Uncle G. will be sending out a search party for us."

Archie didn't need much driving. As soon as he saw all three of his pursuers in the road he gave a loud squawk and flew up the drive towards the house. He had a long start of John, Henry and Noel, who had to enter the drive by the gate, but they ran after him at full speed, Henry a long way in the lead and Noel puffing at the back. Henry was just in time to see Archie's remaining tail feathers disappearing through the dining-room window; he paused for a moment to allow the others to catch up and then they advanced across the lawn in a body to see that the Holbrookes and Christopher had already started dinner and Archie was perched on Mrs. Holbrooke's shoulder. He gave his pursuers a look of contempt and then turning to his mistress he asked affectionately, "Shall we kiss? Oh, *yes*," he answered himself coyly.

CHAPTER SEVEN

Owing to Christopher's timely recovery the much dreaded task of telling the Holbrookes did not have to be performed by Noel, John or Henry. Christopher had told the whole story before dinner. The Major merely said that he hoped everyone had had enough of a fright to make him more sensible in future and Mrs. Holbrooke added that they *must* wear hard hats. Archie's escapade also passed off very agreeably; Mrs. Holbrooke said that Noel, John and Henry were idiots to let him out, but that really it didn't matter a bit and if she had been at home there would have been no trouble about catching him.

After breakfast on Saturday, while the Pony Club members were grooming their ponies and agreeing how peaceful it was without Merry, the Major was talking to Crandall, his farm foreman. As he followed the riders into the paddock, they noticed that he looked rather grim and when he asked if they had been aware that they had spent the morning before spoiling a field of young grass, they knew the reason why.

"Crikey," muttered John, who, being a farmer's son, knew the enormity of the offence.

"Young grass," said the Major, "is delicate stuff; for its first summer it should only be lightly grazed and certainly not galloped over and cut up by a pack of idiotic children, who ought to know better."

"Oh dear," said Noel, and Susan said, "Golly, but I didn't know that anything hurt grass."

"I should have imagined that people who hunt would

have taken the trouble to learn a little about crops," said the Major acidly, "but anyway the deed is done and my foreman tells me that we shall have to take a man and a tractor off harvesting on Monday to roll the field in an attempt to repair the damage."

"I'm terribly sorry, sir," said Dick. "We had no idea—"

"No, none at all," added Harry. "In fact someone asked me if I thought it would be O.K. to ride there and it never entered my head that the field was anything other than ordinary grass."

"Well, perhaps in future, such thoughts will enter your head," said the Major, "and now you are all going to change horses for the first half of this morning's ride. I want Hilary to give Northwind to Noel and fetch the Merry Widow from the stable. Roger and Henry change over. Susan take Sonnet and give Dick Golden Wonder. John, you take Crispin and Turpin back to the stables and bring down Fireworks for June; you're riding Golden Glory."

"Gosh!" said everyone and the people who were pleased with their new mounts—John and Roger, Hilary and Dick—added "Hurray"; the less fortunate groaned, sighed or muttered discontentedly.

"It's very easy to make mistakes about people's riding ability if you always see them on the same horse," the Major explained when everyone had found his right mount and was busily adjusting his stirrups. "I don't like making mistakes and so this morning I'm giving myself an opportunity to correct any that I may be on the verge of making. Lead on round the school, Hilary, please." Everyone was very wide awake as he probed into his new mount's capabilities and character. A few riders hoped that they were giving a better show than the owner usually gave and Hilary felt like a queen on the Merry Widow.

But Noel found no poetry in Northwind's rather stumpy stride; she felt hot and tired and angry with the Major for each time he looked at her his criticism was the same, "Come on, Noel, legs, legs." John was hot and bothered, because Golden Glory was behind the bit as usual and each time he had to ride away from the other horses she began to nap and buck. He could prevent her from going back to the other horses, but he couldn't prevent her from trying to go and the Major said that a good rider, by anticipating his horse, should be able to do so and that John was always too late with his legs. Susan didn't seem able to produce a spark of life from Sonnet and when the Major made remarks about allowing a nice-looking pony to go like something out of a cart, she only groaned and said that honestly she simply *couldn't* use her legs any harder. Henry and Dick both had their mounts going well. Sky Pilot's hocks were underneath him for a change and Wonder was going with more impulsion than she had with Susan and yet more quietly than she went for June. June was having a very strenuous time on Fireworks, but she had more control over him than Christopher and managed him much better than any of the other Pony Club members had expected. Christopher, who had just escaped from breakfast in bed and had come to watch, was quite surprised to see Fireworks stopping at all after all the excitements of the day before.

Noel's legs were beginning to feel as though they might drop off, when the Major gave the order for everyone to change back to his usual mount. Feeling hotter than ever and very disagreeable, she wondered how she could ever have been silly enough to suppose that she might become a good rider? Obviously she was hopeless; she couldn't make Northwind go as well as Hilary could and Sonnet went no worse for Susan. John thought that he would no longer envy June her horse or her prizes. He would rather ride Turpin, any day. June thought, Oh my arms. Thank goodness Glory doesn't pull, but of course I've got good hands. I bet John's spoiled Glory. Roger thought, Henry makes Sky Pilot go better than I do, but he's lucky. I wouldn't mind having the Major as an uncle.

Christopher asked, "Can't I ride now? I'm quite all right honestly, and Fireworks is ready." The Major thought for a little and then he answered that, as the most exhausting half of the morning was over, if Christopher fetched his crash cap he could ride Northwind and Hilary Fireworks, provided, of course, that she had no objection. Hilary said that it would be a pleasure and, in a few moments, everyone was riding round the school again on the appropriate horse. Then the Major ordered half the ride to halt and the first four riders to increase the distance between them to three lengths and then to change the rein at the half pass. Suddenly Noel found that Sonnet was much easier to ride than before; that she was a hundred times easier to ride than Northwind; that really she was going quite well. Plenty of impulsion, thought Noel. Oh, this is a wonderful feeling. "Very good," commented the Major, "but you're still looking down." Everyone's passes were so much better that the Major decided that they could ride the counter change of hand at the half pass. It was perfectly simple, he said. All they had to do, instead of passing diagonally across the whole school, was to ride straight forward for one stride when they reached the centre of the school and then pass in the opposite direction—to the other quarter marker on the side from which they had started. To Noel, who had to go first, it sounded far from simple and she muddled the whole movement horribly, forgetting which was right and which left when the Major began to shout instructions at her. In the end the Major said that Dick had better demonstrate, as he knew from experience that it was hopeless trying to explain school movements to Noel. When everyone had ridden the movement properly, and even Fireworks obliged, the Major said that they would now try the turn on the haunches. "This turn," he said, "is generally taught before passes, but it needs a good deal of tact, if we are not to upset our horse, and I have usually found that if both horse and rider are inexperienced it is better not to teach it too soon. I expect most of you know that the horse pivots on his haunches, his hindlegs marking time on one and the same spot while his forelegs move round in a circle. It is most important that he should step round in quiet even steps and that there should be no attempt to swing him round in a sort of half rear. Come here, Henry. Your horse knows all about it. The aids, which I'm sure you know, are to turn to the left; the rider leads the forehand round with the left rein supported by the right; the right leg, used behind the girth, prevents the quarters swinging to the right and the left leg, on the girth, maintaining the impulsion and prevents the horse stepping back." Black Magic made a perfect turn to either side and Henry sat there looking rather smug while the Major asked, "Has anyone else done it before?"

"I used to on Romany," admitted Noel. "I tried to teach Sonnet, but it didn't seem to work very well, so I gave up."

"Typical," said the Major. "Well, come on, we'll have you next."

"Oh dear, I'm hopeless," said Noel, "and I've forgotten the aids."

"Oh you haven't," said Susan. "You always say that you have, but you don't really forget them."

"But it's quite true, I have forgotten them," objected Noel.

"It isn't," said Susan.

"Stop arguing and bring that pony alongside this hedge," said Major Holbrooke. Noel obeyed reluctantly. "You've seen a schooled horse turn on the haunches, now you're going to see how we teach the turn," the Major told the Pony Club members. "Now Sonnet can't move to the right because of the hedge. Bring your hands to the left, Noel, and feel her mouth enough to prevent her walking forward, press with your right leg. Nothing happens; that's quite usual. Now give her a tap on the right shoulder with your stick; don't let her go forward, or backwards, press her with both legs. She's bound to try to move in every direction but the right one, because she hasn't the faintest idea what these new aids mean and we're going to need quite a lot of patience to teach her. A little more left rein; good, that was only a small step, but it was the right idea. Pat her a lot. Who's next?"

June said, "Glory can do it."

"Oh, she can, can she?" said the Major. "Well come on, let's see her. No, no, no," he added, when June swung Glory round by the reins. "There's no merit in that movement at all. Take that horse beside the hedge and ask her to do one step properly." To everyone's surprise Northwind could do a half turn on the haunches quite nicely, and Christopher was very pleased with him and rewarded him with vast quantities of oats. In between trotting collectedly and extendedly and cantering round the school, they practised turning on the haunches many times that morning and, when the Major said that it was time to jump, everyone could make at least three steps of the turn, which the Major said was quite as much as you should expect from a horse that had never done it before. The members' jumping was very much better than it had ever been, even Fireworks was able to jump three small fences one after the other, though, as the Major pointed out Hilary, having a much stronger seat than Christopher, was better able to stop him. She could pull him up and make him rein-back if he put his weight on his forehand.

"But of course, if you hot him up and gallop him flat out, you can't stop him," said the Major, giving Christopher an evil look, "because he hasn't reached the stage in his schooling when he will come back to hand regardless of what is going on around him."

Tack cleaning was a very hectic time that afternoon. Henry and Christopher—who was supposed to be keeping quiet started throwing tack sponges and saddle soap rags and before long a water fight was waging with Christopher, John and the two Radcliffes against the other five Pony Club members. June was rather aloof until a very wet and soapy sponge, flung by Christopher, caught her full in the face; then she joined in with energy, determined to be revenged. There was a great deal of noise and everyone became very wet, especially when Henry borrowed a garden spray from the tool shed. Of course in the end everyone became too silly. Christopher threw half a bucket of water over June, Henry broke the saddle room window, Hilary's shirt came to bits in Dick's hands and finally the top of the barn tap came off when Noel tried to turn it on. The result was a torrent of water and, when Noel tried to screw the tap together again, it sprayed out in all directions, soaking her to the skin. Dick came running and said that he would have a try, but only succeeded in soaking himself too. Christopher wanted a go; John was sure you turned the tap in a clockwise direction, Hilary was equally sure that the right direction was anti-clockwise. Roger said that there must be some way of getting the ghastly thing on again. All of them had a try and they were all dripping, when Henry said that he was going to fetch Blake to turn the water off at the main. Blake was rather shocked to see so many soaking people and he was even more shocked by the state of his usually immaculate yard. "What a mess," he grumbled. "Whatever have you been doing?"

"Cheer up, Blakie, we'll restore everything to its usual exquisite state of cleanliness before Uncle George sees it," said Henry, screwing up his nose as he bent down to pick up a wet metal polish rag.

"I must go," said June. "Here's Mummy and I'm simply soaked; you are tiresome, Christopher."

"Yes, I know, I'm an awful fool sometimes," said Christopher meekly, "but can't you tell your Ma that you tripped and fell into the tack bucket?"

"Then I should get into a row for being clumsy," said June crossly.

Blake took some time to turn the water off, but once it was done Henry managed to screw the tap together quite easily. Then they spent a dreary quarter of an hour putting away cans and buckets, collecting rags and sponges, sweeping puddles of water towards drains and putting broken glass in the stable dust bin.

"And there's still that awful field," said John when the yard was tidy again. "We shall have to do something about it."

"Oh the young grass," said Henry. "Yes, I'd forgotten about that; we certainly put our foot in it there."

"What sort of tractors does the Major use?" asked John.

"Don't ask me," answered Henry, "all tractors are just tractors to me."

"We have Ferguson's at home," said John. "I drive them quite a bit, but, of course I'm not old enough for a licence yet."

"I think we'd better go and change," said Noel. "We can't have tea like this."

"No, we do look a bit tatty," agreed Henry.

At tea Henry told the Major of his unfortunate accident with the saddle room window and Noel told of hers with the tap. Christopher went as far as describing some of the milder moments of the water fight, which John thought a bit risky, though, luckily, the Holbrookes appeared quite amused.

"But you're drenched, my pet," said Mrs. Cresswell indignantly as she and June drove down the Folly Court drive. "Your clothes are simply saturated, in fact you're wet through. It must have been more than a game, it isn't fun to drench a person to the skin; I'm certain one of those children did it on purpose, out of spite because they don't like you having better riding clothes than any of them; tell me who it was, my pet, and I'll complain to Major Holbrooke; he really can't allow such things to happen right under his nose."

"Oh don't be silly, Mummy," said June sulkily. "I told you it was only in fun."

"You can't call it fun, June," objected her mother. "It's downright spite."

"You are a fool, Mummy," said June.

"Really, June, how many times have I told you that I won't be spoken to in that rude way," stormed Mrs. Cresswell. "I don't know where your nice manners have gone to; it must be Pinelands. If we have any more of this rudeness I shall send you somewhere else."

"I wouldn't care," said June. "You don't know what happened to-day," she went on before her mother had time to speak, "we all changed horses and John Manners rode Glory." June waited with a smug face for the explosion which she knew would follow. Mrs. Cresswell gasped. "That mutton-fisted Manners boy on Glory?" she said in horror. "Was Major Holbrooke there? Did he allow it?" she asked.

"He told us to change," said June. "I had Fireworks and he is a beastly, bad-mannered pony too."

"Major Holbrooke told you to change?" asked Mrs. Cresswell in incredulous accents. "Is this true, June?"

"Of course. Don't be so silly, Mummy," said June. "John may have spoiled her a bit, but there's no need to behave as though the world had ended."

"You only say that because you don't realise Glory's

true worth and the time and trouble I've spent having you taught to ride," said Mrs. Cresswell. "It's simply disgraceful. There might easily have been an accident, for that Manners boy can't ride at all. I can understand the Major wanting you to ride some of the other children's ponies, just to show them how they should go, and they need it, but to put that great stupid Manners boy on Glory—it's, it's—disgraceful; there is no other word for it. Especially after the time I've spent impressing on him that Glory is a very valuable mare. I shall ring him up and complain; it's disgraceful, it really is."

On Sunday the horses all had a rest. Noel, John, Henry and Christopher brought them into the stables, out of reach of the flies, before they went to church, and gave them their feeds. Except for Christopher, who as usual was filled with energy, the Folly Court riders were glad of a rest themselves. After lunch they lay on the lawn and threw daisies at each other until Christopher persuaded them that it would be a good idea to walk to Folly Farm and visit the brood mares and their foals. They asked if they could take the Holbrooke dogs and they collected Lucifer, the black spaniel, and Grit and Grime, the working terriers.

There were three thoroughbred mares with foals in the big loose-boxes at the farm, besides Harmony, the Major's grey Anglo-Arab, which had been champion hack the year before and won many dressage tests; she was supposed to be in foal; and Southwind, a pure-bred Arab, who had a lovely little Arab foal with enormous eyes and a very broad forehead. The foals were all very inquisitive, though rather nervous of strangers, and the Pony Club members talked to them for some time and tried to make up their minds which they liked best. Then they wandered down to the big meadow with the shelter, where the young horses were turned out. There were three yearlings, two two-year-olds and a three-year-old; they were even more inquisitive than the foals and not at all afraid of their visitors. They searched everyone's pockets, ate a green button off Noel's dress and tried to eat Henry's hair, which, as Christopher remarked, did look rather like poor quality meadow hay.

"We might walk back by way of the kennels," suggested Christopher; "the Major says that there are several litters of puppies there and I haven't seen the new kennels, only the old ones at Gunston."

"They're fearfully posh," said Henry, "but it's miles, isn't it?"

"Only Swincombe Bottom," said John, "and you can cut across the fields, but I don't think I'll go, I'm always riding over there with messages about dead cows and hay; I'm going to have a decco at the Major's tractors."

"Oh, John, how can you?" said Noel, "those beastly soulless things."

"Well, I must say I prefer the kennels to the tractors," said Henry. "See you at tea, then, John. We'll take the dogs."

They walked to Swincombe Bottom rather slowly. Henry and Noel discussing books and whether men or women wore the silliest hats; Christopher making rather amateurish hunting noises and drawing all the coverts he could find with Grit and Grime and Lucifer. "No sport and no scent to-day," he complained, catching up at the kennel gates.

Barnes, the huntsman seemed very pleased to show them round. He showed them Priceless's five puppies: Playmate, Puzzle, Promise, Postboy and Porter, Rutland's four daughters: Rosa, Ready, Reckless and Rival, and six small lemon and white puppies the property of Tigress. Then he showed them the twenty-two couple of entered hounds lolling comfortably on their benches, the pudding waiting to be eaten, and the stables with, as yet, only two horses up from grass. They admired the appearance of the hounds and the tidiness of the stables and kennels and then they thanked him and said they must go or they would be late for tea. Barnes said that he hoped to see them all out hunting next season.

John seemed rather miserable at tea, but the others talked merrily, mostly about which Master of Foxhounds swore at the field the most, the Major, Sir Charles Dent, the Master he had succeeded, or Sir William Blount, the Master of the East Barsetshire. The Major said that he swore the most, but Henry said that Sir Charles had a larger vocabulary and Christopher related his experiences at the Boxing Day meet. As soon as everyone had finished, John said that they must turn the horses out and as soon as he was out of earshot of the Holbrookes, he turned to the other Pony Club members and said, "I really have done it this time; I've bust up the whole show."

"Now what have you been up to?" asked Henry.

"Spit it out, John, spit it out," said Christopher, looking at him anxiously.

"Well, you know that I went to look at the tractors," said John miserably. "Well, the Major has got a Ferguson—the same sort as ours—and then in the implement shed I saw a roller and I thought that I might roll the ten-acre field and save the man having to do it to-morrow. I got the tractor out, coupled the roller up and drove it out of the shed quite easily. I thought that the road would be be best way to the ten acre, but I misjudged the gateway—the roller's wider than ours and I've smashed the gate-post and brought down about three yards of wall and I can't turn the tractor or uncouple the roller."

"Lawkes!" said Christopher.

"Oh, dear," said Noel.

"You are *hopeless*——" said Henry.

"But what am I to do?" asked John.

"Why did you touch the beastly thing?" asked Henry.

"I wish I hadn't," answered John despondently. "Do you think I'd better go and tell him? I don't know how to begin."

Henry thought for a minute, then he said, "Look, I'll tell him for you if you like." John brightened a little, "Oh, would you really?" he asked, "that would be terribly decent of you."

"Yes, I know," said Henry shortly. "Look, you all go and turn out the horses and I'll beard the wild beast in its den. That is if you're sure that the damage is irreparable; I mean we couldn't build up the wall, put the tractor away and straighten the gatepost?"

"No," said John. "I tried but the wall's wobbly for miles, the gatepost's smashed and I couldn't unjam the drawbar coupling—I bashed it pretty hard."

"Poor John," said Noel.

"Poor Uncle George," said Henry, "we seem to do a lot of damage between us."

"He'll never have the Pony Club to stay again," said Noel sadly.

"You'd better come up to the house and do your stuff when you've turned out the horses," said Henry to John as he turned back towards the house.

"O.K.," answered John, looking a picture of woe. "Oh why do I always make a mess of everything," he groaned when Henry had gone. "Well, you couldn't help it," said Christopher, "and you were trying to improve the field."

"It's decent of Henry," said John as they reached the stables. "He's very nice really, you know," said Noel, "underneath all his affectations."

"Oh, Uncle, an awful tragedy has befallen us," began Henry, who had decided that a bold approach would be best.

"Don't call me Uncle," answered the Major, "and what have you been doing *now*?"

"Well, actually," said Henry, "for once it wasn't me, but I understand that the farm gatepost is no more and that the wall is rather the worse for wear. John hit it with the roller."

"Hit it with the roller? What the devil was he doing with the roller?" demanded the Major angrily. "How did he get it out?"

"With a tractor," answered Henry.

"He's no business to touch the tractors," said the Major. "What on earth is the boy thinking of? Really, this is the limit."

"Apparently he was going to roll the ten-acre field," explained Henry. "You see he was haunted by remorse for having cut up the young grass. The poor devil was only trying to do a good deed."

"Blast the boy and his good deeds," said the Major. "Where is he? I'll give him a piece of my mind."

"Now, Uncle—I mean Uncle George—you mustn't blow him up," said Henry. "He's fearfully miserable now; he looks as though the world was about to end, and you'll only make his inferiority complex worse. Honestly, he's frightfully sorry about the whole thing and he cared much more about the field being spoiled than anyone else."

"I thought that you couldn't stand him," said the Major, looking sharply at Henry. "You've spent most of the last week quarrelling and fighting with each other."

"Well, I couldn't stand him at first," said Henry slowly, "but now I'm getting used to him, he's not at all bad really. His inferiority complex makes him a bit touchy, but he's very reliable, you know that he wouldn't do the dirty on you."

"I see," said the Major, "so you offered to deal with me?"

"Well, he was all of a dither. Didn't you notice his miserable state at tea?" asked Henry.

"Well, where is this wretched child?" said the Major. "Go and fetch him. We shall have to walk up to the farm and look at the damage."

Henry found John sitting on the front doorstep; he wore a very dejected air. "Hallo," said Henry, and then he added in a stage whisper: "He's got over the swearing stage. Come on, we're going to inspect the damage."

"Is he absolutely furious?" asked John.

"Yes," answered the Major, who had come into the hall, "he is."

"I'm terribly sorry, sir," said John, looking embarrassed as well as dejected.

"I told my wife that this would happen if we had the Pony Club to stay," said Major Holbrooke, "but she insisted. Let it be a warning to you, Henry, if you marry, never let your wife persuade you into anything."

John decided that Henry couldn't have told the Major everything or he would be much more angry, so his heart sank lower and lower as they drew near to Folly Farm. The Major was giving Henry a lecture on crop rotation, to which John didn't listen at all. When they reached the farm the wall looked worse than ever to John; there seemed to be thousands of bricks lying everywhere. Henry said, "You did have a smash up."

The Major surveyed the scene for a moment and then he said, "It looks as though we shall have to teach the Pony Club brick laying, instead of dressage. Well, we'd better pile these bricks up, then we might be able to turn the tractor. Henry, run up to the second cottage and ask Jeffrys to come and give us a hand, please; it's his week-end on."

When Henry had gone the Major turned to John. "I've no doubt that your intentions were excellent," he said, "but you really mustn't borrow other people's property without asking, something always happens if you do, and supposing, instead of breaking down a few yards of wall, you had smashed a thousand pounds worth of tractor; then how would you feel about it? Yes, you *must* always ask," he added as Henry and Jeffrys appeared.

It was nearly dinner time when the bricks had been piled neatly inside the farmyard and the roller and tractor uncoupled, with considerable difficulty, turned round and driven back into their appropriate sheds.

Mrs. Holbrooke, Noel and Christopher were in the library when the Major, John and Henry came in from their tidying up. Mrs. Holbrooke was very tactful; she handed her husband a glass of sherry before she asked if they had managed to restore order or told him that Mrs. Cresswell had telephoned twice while he was out and had asked him to ring her as soon as he came in.

"What on earth does *she* want?" asked the Major rather irritably. "Well, I can't ring her now; it's dinner time and I must wash; she'll have to wait till later," and he disappeared upstairs.

After dinner the Major, looking rather pleased with himself, came into the library, where Mrs. Holbrooke and the Pony Club members were talking and drinking coffee. "I seem to have put my foot in it this time," he said. "Mrs. Cresswell's fuming with rage. Apparently I've been allowing all and sundry to ride her wonderful mare, which is now irretrievably spoiled." "What did you say?" asked Mrs. Holbrooke. "I told her a few hard truths," answered the Major, "which weren't very well received and then she suggested that June should give up learning dressage—she knew the whole business anyway and found it so disheartening being kept back because the other kiddies were so far behind. I said that I entirely agreed and that I had noticed her lack of enthusiasm. So there you are except, oh yes, there was one other grievance. It seems that some wicked, spiteful Pony Club member deliberately poured a bucket of water over June yesterday afternoon, drenching her to the skin."

"Oh what a lie!" said Christopher hotly. "It was only half a bucket, honestly; wasn't it, John?"

No one could help laughing.

CHAPTER EIGHT

On Monday morning the dressage class, with no June and no Merry, appeared very much smaller. None of the other Pony Club members seemed to care, in fact several people remarked that it was a good thing. Henry grumbled that June had never made an original remark but always repeated your own back to you in a slightly different form. Dick said that she was a walking catalogue of cups and prizes, and the Radcliffes complained that she had adenoids and said that Mrs. Cresswell ought to ask their father to operate.

When the usual preliminary schooling had been gone through, the Major called all the Pony Club members into the centre of the school and began: "We have now arrived at the canter. The most difficult pace, though few people realise it, at which to ride correctly and also the most difficult pace for the horse; it is *impossible* for a young or badly balanced horse to canter properly. If you try to force your horse to canter slowly before he has acquired the necessary balance he will learn to pull, to headshake or to potter along behind the bit, which quite a number of people mistake for the collected canter.

"Our horses all canter round the school quite comfortably now, they are well enough balanced for that, so we may go on to the next stage; using half the school, endless circling and the starts at the canter. Just as it needs better balance to canter round half the school than round the whole it is easier for our horse to canter large circles than small ones, therefore we begin with large ones and when he does these well we try slightly smaller ones. But, before we begin our circling there is another point I should like to talk about. The canter is a pace of three time; that sounds complicated, but it isn't, it merely means that there are three distinct hoof-beats and what is called the silent time when the horse is in the air, in other words he has no legs on the ground. Supposing that we tell our horse to canter with the near fore leading, the first hoof of which he actually puts to the ground is the off hind, then the off fore and the near hind together—making one beat, and finally the near fore or leading leg. He then swings forward off the leading leg into the air and then down with the off hind to begin the sequence again. Does everyone understand that? It's quite easy. Choose your leading leg, the first leg to the ground is the diagonally opposite hind leg, then the two odd legs, then the leading leg, into the air and begin all over again. Got it?"

"Yes," answered Henry. "I think so," said Noel doubtfully. "Oh golly," said Susan.

"We must now go back to the trot," said Major Holbrooke, "from which pace we are going to ask our horse to canter. As you all know the trot is a movement of two time, the horse puts his off fore and near hind to the ground simultaneously and then changes his weight to the near fore and off hind. If we wish to canter with the near fore leading we apply our aids when the left diagonal, that is near fore and off hind, is in the air or in other words when we see the near foreleg swinging out in front of us for then we know that the horse is about to bring his off hind to the ground and, therefore, will be ready to lead off smoothly into a canter. Does everyone understand that?" asked the Major. "Don't be afraid to say if I haven't made it clear." The Pony Club members were all muttering and trying to work out diagonals with their own hands and legs. "I've got it," said Roger, "it's not half as difficult as it sounds."

"It's all right in theory," said Hilary, "but I don't know what will happen when we try to put it into practice."

"I think I understand," said Susan.

"Well, if no one's any questions we'll see what happens in practice," said the Major. "Lead on round the school at a slow trot, please, Hilary." When everyone was trotting round with his horse fairly awake, Major Holbrooke told Hilary to prepare to canter on the off fore and asked her when she would give the aid, "As I see the off foreleg," answered Hilary. "Quite right," said the Major; "carry on." Everyone had a turn and no one found it very difficult, except Noel, who would look down, and Christopher, who couldn't persuade Fireworks to go on the off leg at all. The Major told Noel that a quick glance should be enough to tell her which diagonal was in the air and, in time, she must learn to tell by feel. To Christopher he said that knowing which diagonal you were on was a great help in making a difficult horse canter on a leg which he disliked, as, if you gave the aid at the right moment, he had to take another stride before he could start on the wrong leg and therefore all you had to do was to prevent him from taking another stride in fact, to give a harder leg aid. When Fireworks had cantered on the off leg, the Major divided the members into two rides, one on either side of the school. They cantered round and at the Major's command circled inwards, each ride turning just short of the centre line and circling back to the outside of the school. Northwind still hadn't enough impulsion and, but for hard work on Hilary's part, he would have dropped back to a trot. Fireworks began by going much too fast but gradually he learned to suit his pace to the size of the circle. Susan would try to make Wonder canter slowly by pulling on the reins with the result that she was either too close to the person in front or else she was trotting. Noel, on the other hand, was concentrating so hard on using her legs and seat that she was always late in obeying the order to circle and usually became muddled up with the person next to her, either John or Hilary, both of whom were annoyed at having their circles spoiled. It was very exhausting work and when both riders and horses were showing signs of collapse the Major called everyone into the centre again and told the riders to dismount and loosen their horses' girths. "I'm afraid that I've got a lot more to say about the canter," he said apologetically. Christopher said, "Lawks!" and Dick said, "I expect we shall survive it."

"The change of leg, as you all know, merely means that you change from one leading leg to the other, because it is dangerous to take sharp corners on the wrong leg, that is with the outside leg leading. In the beginning of our schooling we always pull our horse up to a trot and tell him to strike off on the other leg, but this wastes time and so it is important that a hunter should learn to change legs at the canter when he changes his direction without any signal from his rider. He must change legs behind as well as in front, if he fails to do so he is cantering disunited, which is a very uncomfortable feeling. Then there is the change of leg on a straight line, which is much more difficult and belongs to advanced dressage. The horse must change legs when he is in the air during the fourth or silent time and the aid to change—which is simply to lead on the other leg—is applied during the third-time when you see his forelegs swinging forward to touch the ground. To teach the change of leg we first concentrate on obtaining a fairly slow, well-balanced canter and then on making quite sure that our horse understands the aids for either leg. To do this we practise the consecutive and alternate starts. We've practised the consecutive ones, you remember, cantering so many strides, pulling up and starting off again on the same leg. Now the horses, except Fireworks, are ready to practise the alternate kind, cantering a few strides on either leg while going round the school in either direction, but always being careful to pull up if you are on the wrong leg for a corner, for they are not nearly ready to learn the counter lead—cantering on the wrong leg on purpose. Do not always canter first on one leg and then on the other or twice on one leg and then twice on the other for horses are very quick to notice such things and you might find that your horse was following a routine instead of obeying your orders. Now I want everyone to mark himself out a school, with four sticks or large stones, in this field or the next one and school for the next half-hour, everyone, except Christopher, concentrating mainly on the alternate starts. Christopher, you can practise consecutive starts, circling at all paces and anything else you like. I'm going to school Nothing Ventured over a few fences; I'll answer any questions after lunch."

"Lawks," said Christopher when the Major had gone. "Well, I bags the farthest corner of the next field for my school and no one's to come near."

For a short time everyone schooled busily. Susan was the first person to stop. She rode across to Henry's school, which was next to hers, and asked, "What do you do when your horse can do it, Henry?"

"Go on doing it," answered Henry rather out of breath, for he had just had to quell a sudden desire of Black Magic's to change legs whenever she came near Wonder, "then she'll do it better."

"Oh," said Susan rather abashed and she rode back to her own school and began again. Dick stopped next. "Crispin's worn out," he said to John, "but after all what can you expect, the poor fellow's eighteen now."

"My legs ache," said John, pulling up.

"No slacking there," yelled Roger across the field.

"If you'd been using your legs properly, *you'd* be worn out," shouted John in reply.

"Hear, hear," said Henry. "Mine are in a terrible state, but we've only been schooling for about five minutes—we can't stop yet."

"I've no intention of stopping," said Dick. "I'm just giving Crispin a breather."

"I suppose we ought to practise peaceful things in between the strenuous work," said Henry.

"I'm terribly bad at the turn on the haunches," said John. "I just don't seem able to get the hang of it."

"Would you like a try on Black Magic?" offered Henry. "She's an absolute artist at it and I think it's a help if you know the feel."

"Thanks awfully," said John. "Would you like to try Turpin? I expect you'll get him to do it much better than I can." They changed horses. John found that Black Magic made a perfect turn while Henry persuaded Turpin to make half a turn to either side, standing alongside the hedge.

"Can you do a half pass at the trot?" Hilary asked Dick. She had been trying to persuade a reluctant Northwind to do one without much success.

"We haven't got to do that yet, have we?" asked Dick.

"No," answered Hilary, "but I heard the Major muttering that we were going to try them to-morrow."

Noel and Christopher were still schooling busily in the next field when the other members decided that it was time for lunch. "Let's have a race to them," suggested Roger. But Dick said, "I've had enough races to last me for a long time." So they crossed the field cantering fifteen strides on each leg in turn.

"Come on," shouted Henry. "It's lunch time." Susan said, "I don't know how you two can keep on doing the same old thing for so long."

Christopher answered, "I haven't been doing the same thing." And Noel said, "I've got to if I want Sonnet to improve." They cantered back across the field towards the gate to the stable yard. Fireworks, realising that he was going home, began to pull; Golden Wonder began to gallop; the other horses and ponies were racing each other. Fireworks and Wonder stopped dead at the gate, shooting their riders up their necks. All the Pony Club members were laughing. The Major was standing at the gate; he had come to say that it was time for lunch, but now he said, "There's a very old rule about walking the first half-mile and the last half-mile—unless it's raining—which also applies to schooling. Apart from the importance of bringing your horse in cool, it is always very bad policy to canter towards the stable at the end of your ride; it encourages nappiness. Take them all away again and walk them in and then hurry up with the feeding or you'll be late for lunch."

"O.K.," said the Pony Club members, feeling rather abashed.

After lunch Major Holbrooke remembered to ask if anyone had any questions. Most of the members said no firmly, but Susan wanted to know how long you ought to go on doing a thing after your horse knew it. The Major answered that that depended on the thing. The turn on the forehand, for instance, wasn't in itself a useful movement; it was used to teach a young horse obedience to the leg, and when the horse obeyed the leg one gave up practising that turn. But all movements which improved a horse's balance and suppleness could be practised indefinitely. "Does that answer your question?" he asked.

"In a way," answered Susan, "but I meant how long should you go on doing a thing each time you school?"

"Well, there again, it depends a great deal on the thing. Anything which is an effort to the horse should not be done more than a couple of times in one lesson, because we do not want to upset him or sicken him of his work.

Big fences, for instance, should only be jumped once during a lesson unless the horse makes a mistake, then you must put him over again. The smaller the fence and the less effort it is to your horse the more often you may jump it. Mix up your schooling, that will prevent both you and your horse from becoming bored; don't spend twenty minutes on extended and collected trotting followed by ten minutes turning on the haunches, or the horse will go to sleep; use your turn on the haunches as a method of changing your direction, change the rein by passing across the school; keep your horse alert by constant changes of direction, pace and gait. Any more questions?"

Noel asked, in rather a dreary voice, what you should do if you found that your horse was getting worse and worse instead of better. This sent the other Pony Club members into fits of giggles.

"Horses have their good days and bad ones, like anyone else," said Major Holbrooke, "but if a horse of mine began to get worse and worse I should consider his schooling, whether I had overdone it or hurried him; his health, was he eating all right, having enough oats and were his legs filling at all? If it didn't seem to be due to any of these things I should give him several days quiet hacking and then hope for an improvement. But, if I were you, Noel, and I was convinced that my horse was getting worse and that it wasn't my imagination, I should ride over and ask my long-suffering friend, Major Holbrooke, what was wrong." "O.K.," said Noel, "I will."

"You don't know what you've let yourself in for, Uncle George," said Henry. "She'll call on you at least once a week."

"That will be a pleasure," said the Major. "And now, if there aren't any more questions, you'd better clean your tack, because I've got a painting job I want done—the dressage markers are looking a bit the worse for wear and

I want to mark out the arena to-morrow so that everyone can ride in it before the test."

"Test?" said the Pony Club members in rather dismayed accents.

"What test?" asked Henry.

"The dressage test, of course," answered the Major, hurrying away.

The Pony Club members looked at each other. "I don't like the sound of it," said John.

"He's the limit, springing it on us like this," said Henry indignantly.

"Golly, I shan't remember a thing," said Susan.

"It might be quite fun," said Hilary. "I don't mind riding tests as long as there isn't an oral section."

"There won't be any oral," said Noel. "At least, not if it's a proper dressage test." "Well, what happens?" asked Susan.

"Oh you know: 'Enter at the ordinary trot at X halt and salute. At C track right K serpentine,' " said Noel and then she moaned, "Oh dear, I've got the needle already."

"Oh, you *can't* have," objected Susan. "You've only just been told."

The tack was cleaned very much more quickly and not much worse than usual that afternoon and then the Pony Club members routed out Major Holbrooke, and demanded paint and brushes. The markers were biscuit tins painted white with the same letter in black on all four sides. There was plenty of paint but only five brushes, three for white paint and two for black. "You'll need steady hands for the lettering," said the Major, "and don't get yourselves covered in paint."

Of course everyone wanted to paint and three people couldn't. "I bags a brush," said John. "I'm going to do lettering, because I've got a steady hand," said Henry. The two Radcliffes grabbed brushes. "This isn't fair," said

Christopher indignantly, "there's only one left between four of us."

"Well, toss for it," suggested John.

"We shall have to take it in turns," said Dick.

"O.K.," said Hilary, "someone can have my brush when I've finished this tin."

They tossed up for the remaining brush—a white one—and Noel won. Christopher soon became tired of watching the painters; he collected Grit and Grime and took them round behind the muck heap and the hay barn to look for rats. Dick lay on his back on the grass plot in the middle of the yard; Susan gave Noel good advice. Presently Noel finished D's background and offered her brush to Susan; then she dropped D on the grass and his immaculate background was speckled with blades of grass and bits of dust. "Oh dear," she said, "he's ruined."

"Try the turps rag," suggested Henry, throwing it across to her.

"No, leave it alone; the muck'll all come off when it's dry," said Roger.

"What a hope," said Noel despondently. Then Roger got up to fetch another marker and tripped over the black paint pot. "Oh, blast," he said, as the paint ran all over the gravel, "quick, where's the lid?" He tried to scoop the paint back into the pot, but he wasn't very successful, merely getting it all over his hands. "Dip in your brushes," he told the others, "I don't want to waste more than I need."

They painted in silence for some time after this, until Roger felt something sticking into his back, and turned to find Christopher behind him. "What do you think you're doing?" he demanded angrily.

"Nothing," answered Christopher with a grin which contradicted his words. The other members looked round to see that he had painted a large black P.O.W. across Roger's shirt.

"Oh, you filthy little beast," said Henry. "You'll cop it when Roger sees what you've done."

"What has he done?" asked Roger, twisting round. "Oh, you've been writing on me," he said, catching sight of the stick in Christopher's hand. "You wait till I catch you." Christopher threw down the stick and ran; Roger tore after him.

"We've nearly enough paint brushes now," said Henry. "And someone can have mine; I've done two markers," said John, getting to his feet and wandering off.

Roger caught Christopher in the kitchen garden and ducked him head first in the water butt by way of revenge. Meanwhile the other Pony Club members managed to finish the painting in peace and then they wandered off in search of John. Roger joined them, but Christopher dashed indoors to wash his hair which was green and rather slimy. They found John loading straw bales in the barley field. "What energy," remarked Henry in a languid voice.

"Well, come on, do some work," said John.

"It'll get our weight down for the Hunter Trials," said Dick, thinking of Crispin.

The Pony Club members worked hard that evening and when it was time for the Radcliffes, Dick and Susan to go home, the Major produced several bottles of cider, which were very well received. Christopher and Susan soon began to giggle and say that they were drunk, but when Roger offered to sober Christopher by ducking him in the garden water butt again, he stopped giggling at once and said that they must turn out the ponies as he wanted to have a bath before dinner. Henry said, "Good lord! A bath? What on earth's come over you, Christopher?" for he was known to dislike them, but Christopher answered that he had prickles inside his shirt, dust all over him, that his hair still smelled funny and that Henry could shut up.

On Tuesday the dressage arena had to be laid out. Major Holbrooke produced a plan, an enormously long tape measure, a scientific method for working out right-angles and one hundred and thirty-two yard-long white boards which slotted together to make the surround.

Hilary and Roger measured, John wrote the centre line letters X and G in whitewash on the appropriate spots, Henry argued with his Uncle about the best way to work out right-angles and the rest of the members crawled round setting up the boards.

When at last the arena was ready with the newly painted letters in position round the outside, the Major told the Pony Club members his plans for the next four days.

"Tomorrow," he said, "we are going to have a practice hunter trial and decide who is going to enter for what on Saturday. On Thursday we have our dressage test and on Friday we box the horses down to Colonel Shellbourne's, where we are all spending the night. How he proposes to fit us all in, I don't know, but he insists on having us. On Saturday night we all come back here and those of you who are not staying at Folly Court had better tell your parents not to expect you until they see you. Ponies, tack and people staying at Folly Court are not expected to leave until Sunday afternoon at the earliest—Monday if you like. Now is that clear?"

"Yes," answered the Pony Club members and Noel only just prevented herself from saying that her needle was worse than ever.

"I hope that we don't lose your ten pounds for you, Uncle George," said Henry, "but it'll be a near thing if you ask me."

"You underestimate my teaching ability," said Major Holbrooke. "I've already decided how to spend it."

CHAPTER NINE

THE morning of the hunter trial practice was grey and damp. A light drizzle fell as the Pony Club members groomed their ponies.

"It would be awful if it really poured and we couldn't jump," said Christopher.

"One jumps at hunter trials whatever the going—unless, of course, they're cancelled—so I don't see why one shouldn't *practise* on slippery ground," said Henry.

"Well, I'm sure that it's not going to rain hard," said Hilary firmly.

The Major's course was quite a long one. Henry said that it was well over a mile, but the Major said that he was exaggerating. There were four hedges without ditches, two with them on the take off and one with a ditch on the landing side. There were two fairly stout flights of posts and rails, a very narrow stile in the corner of a field and two flights of hurdles making an in and out. The Major sent everyone to walk the course and then he said that the fourteen hand ponies were to jump first and that he would raise the rails for the two horses. John offered to go first and the Major started him with instructions to go a fair hunting pace and keep between the flags; he made a clear round. Fireworks, who was started next, galloped round at a tremendous speed, but he knocked down the top bar of the stile. Wonder cleared all the jumps, but the Major said that she hadn't galloped fast enough; Susan was too inclined to ride at a collected canter between the fences. Dick and Crispin made a very good round, but Noel was told that she was feeble, because she let Sonnet refuse the first fence. After that she used her legs frantically and Sonnet cleared everything, but Noel could feel that she lacked confidence and was afraid of the flags.

"She'll be all right," said the Major, when Noel told him. "She needs experience and you *must* use your legs."

Northwind cleared all the jumps, but he wouldn't hurry himself because he knew that there were no hounds and he didn't believe in hurrying except out hunting. The Major offered to fetch his hunting horn and try to wake him up with, but Christopher shrieked and said that a horn would send Fireworks mad. John rode across and put up the rails and then the Major started Henry. Black Magic made an enormous jump over the first fence, because she noticed the ditch at the last moment, and Henry fell off. His uncle told him unsympathetically that it was his own fault for having his knees out. Henry—who hadn't hurt himself—merely grinned, caught Black Magic and finished the course without any more mistakes. Roger and Sky Pilot crashed the stile, which, the Major said, was Roger's fault, because he hadn't used his brains. He should have collected his horse for such a difficult jump, not ridden at it anyhow. Sky Pilot and Fireworks were both sent to jump the stile again, and when they returned the Major asked if anyone particularly wanted to go with anyone else in the pair class. "Obviously," he said, "the two horses will have to go together and I think they'll make quite a good pair; but all the ponies are about the same size so we can try any two you like."

"Will you come with me, Dick?" asked John.

"No one will want to go with me," said Christopher rather miserably. "I'm sure to let them down."

"I'll go with you if you don't mind if I let *you* down," said Noel.

"Who am I to go with?" asked Susan.

"I'll start the horses while you argue it out," said Major

Holbrooke. "Don't jump the stile," he told Roger and Henry, "it's too narrow; take that nice piece of hedge on the left, there's a small ditch on the landing side, so mind that you don't come off."

"O.K.," said Henry, pulling up his stirrups a hole and putting his knees in very firmly. "We'll do our best. Which side do you want, Roger?"

"You go on the outside," said Roger. "You're the faster. Who's going to shout when we're to push on?"

"You," said Henry.

Roger and Henry kept together very well, once Henry had realised that Black Magic's acceleration was much faster than Sky Pilot's and that he mustn't give her her head immediately Roger said, "*Now.*"

Hilary and Susan were still arguing about whether they should be a pair or whether it would be better for Susan to go with Noel, when the horses came back. The Major said that he had never known people so hopeless at deciding anything and that he thought it would be much better if the two who were slow made one pair, and the unknown element, which was Fireworks and Sonnet, did the best they could.

John and Dick were an excellent pair. Their ponies seemed to understand what they were supposed to be doing and they kept together without any effort on the part of their riders. Northwind and Golden Wonder were not so good. Susan seemed unable to keep Wonder going at a steady pace; either she cantered collectedly or—when Hilary shrieked "faster"—she galloped flat out and Northwind could not keep up. The Major sent them to practise cantering round a field together and then he said that Noel and Christopher could start and that they were to keep calm and not to go too fast. Noel, determined not to let Sonnet refuse the first fence again, rode her very hard and she cleared it easily. Christopher was forging ahead, Noel urged Sonnet forward and they galloped across the field. "Is this all right for you?" shrieked Christopher, "I can't go any slower." "It's O.K.," answered Noel. Sonnet was evidently faster than she had thought her. It was as they came back towards the start that disaster overtook them. They were going really fast and both ponies were jumping well, taking off early and landing right out in the next field. Then at the hedge, which they were jumping instead of the stile, Fireworks jumped even bigger, for he saw the ditch on the far side; as he landed his girth slipped back and he began to buck, first from irritation and then, as the saddle slipped back on his loins and the girth flapped round his stifles, from terror. Christopher was helpless; he could neither use his legs nor pull on the reins. "Get off," shrieked Noel, who was unable to persuade Sonnet to approach the frightened pony, and the Major, who was hurrying across the next field, echoed her cry. Christopher half-jumped and half-fell off and then he rolled away from Fireworks. The saddle slipped right round under Fireworks' tummy and flapped between his hind legs. Terrified, Fireworks shot across the field, bucking furiously, and charged the hedge; he fell and lay for a moment on his back in the ditch; both the stirrups came off. Noel rode towards him, but he was on his feet again kicking frantically with both hind legs. "Keep away," shouted the Major, but Sonnet had no intention of approaching those flying hoofs; she refused to go forward. Suddenly, Fireworks, finding that bucking would not free him of this fearful clinging thing, set off at a purposeful gallop. He jumped the hedge out of the field and took the track across the fields to the farm. Noel followed and the other Pony Club members started in pursuit. Sonnet galloped at full speed but Fireworks had taken the stout five-barred gate in his stride; Noel had to jump two hedges to avoid it; Fireworks had jumped the iron gate into the farmyard: Noel had to stop and open it. Three farm workers stood white-faced and open-mouthed.

"Which way did he go?" shouted Noel.

"Down the 'Ogshill road," they answered.

So Noel turned left and then right and took the Hogshill road. She cantered along the grass verge; she knew that Fireworks would be leaving her farther and farther behind, but it would be foolhardy to go any faster, she told herself; two horses with broken knees would be worse than one. But the thought of motor accidents made her go as fast as she dared; poor Christopher, she thought, supposing Fireworks was killed? Poor Fireworks! She cantered past the archway which marked the entrance to the Priory—if only he would have turned in, but the white slip marks led on, leaving no doubts, long white slip marks made by galloping iron-shod hoofs. She reached the famous Hogshill, so steep that many riders led their horses down it and everyone took the other road to Gunston if they could. Surely Fireworks had not galloped down? Surely no horse could gallop and stand up on its glass-like surface? But the slip marks led on. Noel rode Sonnet at an extended trot down the narrow footpath which was raised about eight feet above the road. I hope I don't meet a pram, she thought. She turned the last bend, expecting to see Fireworks lying in a crumpled heap at the bottom of the hill, but the slip marks still led on and the little village of Hogshill was in a great state of excitement. "Go on! Go on!" they shouted from their gates as Noel clattered through; "He's galloping towards Gunston!" they shrieked from upstairs windows. Children gazed with goggling eyes, dogs yapped hysterically. Noel rode into Matchetts, the suburbs of Gunston. Semi-detached Tudor-style residences bordered the road. " 'E's gone over the bridge," yelled a small boy on a bicycle. Noel remembered that the river and the toll gate still separated her from Gunston. If only the toll gates were shut, but as she turned the corner she saw that they stood open and the man who collected the tolls was looking up the road to Gunston. "Has a loose pony gone through?" asked Noel as she trotted by him. "Yes," he answered. "Straight on to Gunston."

Sonnet didn't like the bridge; she peered apprehensively at the water below, but Noel used her legs and they trotted on and came to where the railway bridge made a tunnel over the road. Sonnet thought this even worse than the river one; she began to shy and stop; Noel could hear a train coming, she used her legs frantically and they shot through hastened by the echoing clank of Sonnet's shoes. The train rumbled over behind them, causing Sonnet to career up the road. West Street, Gunston's second busiest street, lay ahead. Cars and buses, bicycles and pedestrians hurried up and down it. Where was Fireworks? There *must* have been an accident, thought Noel.

"Have you seen a loose pony?" she asked a group of people at the corner. "He went straight over," they answered, pointing at a gravel road. Noel heaved a sigh of relief, at least he hadn't gone on into the centre of the town. She crossed the street, holding up the traffic, and cantered along the gravelled road. She could see Fireworks' hoofmarks and she realised that she was behind Gunston station. The road led up to the goods yard and, by a stroke of good fortune, the tall iron gate at the top was shut and she rounded the corner to see Fireworks standing a dejected, sweat-covered figure with heaving sides and hanging head. "Poor old man," said Noel, dismounting and walking up to him. The saddle still hung upside down, but he was too tired to care any more. She took the reins over his head; they weren't broken. She looked at his legs, which were covered in blood; it was difficult to tell exactly how badly he had hurt himself, but she could see no really serious wounds and his knees were untouched She tied both ponies to the fence and straightened Fireworks' saddle; it was covered in blood and the cantle seemed rather battered. "I wonder if you're lame?" said Noel to Fireworks as she led both ponies down the road, but he didn't seem to be and so she mounted Sonnet. "Christopher will be pleased," she told the ponies. Sonnet was tired, but she was also longing to be back at Folly Court, so she and Fireworks both insisted on jogging down the road. All the people in West Street stared as Noel crossed it with two ponies, but they didn't say anything. The man at the toll gates said, "You got him then," but he didn't demand any money for tolls, which was just as well for Noel had none on her. The small boy on the bicycle was still pedalling up and down the road, he stopped to stare. "She's caught 'im," he said to no one in particular as Noel rode past. The inhabitants of Hogshill village were still at their gates and looking out of their windows and they all turned as they heard the sound of hoofs coming up the road. "She's got 'im," they said to each other, and "Look at all the blood on his saddle; there must have been an accident." The ponies tackled the Hogshill valiantly but by the time they had reached the top and were turning up the Folly Court drive, Sonnet was beginning to droop. Fireworks, however, was not behaving at all like an invalid and he jogged and pulled as they entered the stable yard.

There was a shriek of "Here she is, and she's got him," from Susan; Dick and the Radcliffes rushed out of the saddle room. "Is he hurt?" Blake bustled up as Noel dismounted. "It looks awful," said Noel, "but I don't think he's seriously hurt."

"'E's been very lucky," said Blake, bending to look at each leg in turn, "very lucky. Will you take 'im into the box next to Black Magic?" he asked Hilary. "I'll just get some warm water and antiseptic." Noel patted Sonnet and said, "You seem to have cooled off now, you must have an extra big feed for lunch. Where's Christopher?" she asked Susan as they led Sonnet to the barn. "He's in the car with John and Henry and the Major," explained Susan. "I don't know why you didn't meet them, but I suppose they took the other road. The Major said that there was no point in any more of us persuing you, so we had to come back and miss all the fun."

"Fun!" said Noel. "I didn't think it was fun; tearing along slippery roads, expecting to fall down at any minute and to find a corpse round every corner."

"Well, it was awful staying behind," said Susan.

"I wish Christopher would come back," said Noel. "Everyone along the Hogshill road saw me, so if he asks he'll be told I've got Fireworks."

"I wonder if he'll be all right for the hunter trials," said Susan.

"Oh, I hope so," said Noel. "And I hope Sonnet will be for that matter. All that tearing along roads can't have done her any good. Do you think she'll throw a splint?" she asked anxiously. "After all, she's only five."

"No, I'm sure she won't," said Susan in a comfortably convincing voice.

When the car party had returned and inspected Fireworks, the Major said what he had refrained from saying until he knew that the pony was in one piece, that, in future, Christopher would remember to tighten his girths. In answer to anxious inquiries whether Sonnet and Fireworks would be rideable next day, he said that time would show and that Fireworks must spend the night in the stable so that the flies would not worry his numerous scrapes and cuts.

After lunch, which was late, and tack cleaning which took even longer than usual owing to everyone relating his version of Fireworks' mishap and his thoughts and feelings while in pursuit, Major Holbrooke appeared with eight neatly typewritten documents, which he handed round to the Pony Club members.

"What on earth?" said Roger, looking at his in a suspicious manner.

"Lawks!" said Christopher.

"It's the dressage test," said Noel excitedly. "We've got to learn it by heart," she added in more subdued tones.

"What?" said Henry in horror.

"Oh, I say, look here, sir," said Dick, "this is a bit much."

"Uncle," said Henry, "you don't really expect us to learn all this A B business by heart, do you?"

"I do indeed," said Major Holbrooke, looking rather smug. "Surely I haven't overrated your intelligence? It's not a very difficult test and you have the rest of the day to learn it."

"But we've never practised," said Hilary.

"What have you been doing for the past ten days then?" asked the Major. "I quite thought that you were in my dressage class. I must be getting short-sighted in my old age."

"But we never had a dressage *test*," said Hilary.

"You were learning dressage," said the Major, "tomorrow we're having a test to see how accurately and with what degree of brilliance you can carry out the movements which you have been learning and practising for the past ten days."

"Oh," said Hilary.

"Even if one is entering for a real competition, one only goes through the whole test consecutively a few times for one's own benefit, because to do it too often is bad for the horse; he begins to anticipate the movements."

"But I'm sure I can't learn all this, honestly," said John in dismayed accents.

"Nor me," said Susan. "It's all very well for Noel and

Henry, they're always spouting poetry—they can learn by heart—I never get more than 'fair' for learning anything at school."

"They'll be astounded when you start getting 'excellent' next term then," said the Major, "the brain is only a muscle, you know."

Susan giggled, "We don't have 'excellent' at my school," she said, "the best you can get is 'very good'."

Folly Court was very peaceful that evening. Henry, Noel, John and Christopher sat at the nursery table or sprawled on the floor in attitudes of intense concentration. Occasionally they leapt to their feet and paced round the room halting at X or changing the rein from M to K. "I do hope Fireworks'll be all right," said Christopher suddenly, "I should like to have a go."

"Ssh," said John, and Noel said, "I'll lend you Sonnet."

CHAPTER TEN

CHRISTOPHER was up long before anyone else at Folly Court on the morning of the dressage test. He felt very despondent when he saw the size of Fireworks' legs; "I'm sure I shan't be able to ride you to-day," he told him. "I can only hope you'll be ready for Saturday. Oh, I am a fool; why didn't I tighten my girths?" However, despondency didn't seem to be much use, so he began to muck out Fireworks' loose-box. By the time that he had bedded him down on vast quantities of clean straw, filled up his water bucket and fetched him some hay, Blake, Victor and Fred were all at work. Christopher asked Blake for cod liver oil cake and bran, the Holbrooke's cook for some carrots and collected a few sowthistles of which Fireworks was extremely fond. Fireworks was delighted with his breakfast, he ate the lot with great relish and seemed to enjoy being an invalid.

The Major was out in the stable yard before breakfast and Christopher greeted him with, "His legs are awfully swelled and Blake says that he won't be able to do dressage."

"Good morning," said the Major. "Well, we expected some swelling. One can't gallop to Gunston, jumping a couple of gates en route, and expect to get off scot free."

"There's nothing much wrong with 'im, sir," said Blake, joining them at the loose-box door. "'E'll be all right for Saturday."

"But not to-day, you think?" said the Major. "I expect you're right; he's bound to be stiff, particularly after a night in the stable. Well, we must find you something else to ride, Christopher, and you'd better take Fireworks for a walk after breakfast."

"I know it's silly," Noel was saying to John as they entered the dining-room, "but honestly I've got such awful needle I don't feel like eating a thing."

"No breakfast, no dressage," said Major Holbrooke firmly, "and please remember," he went on, "that there is no need to take this test seriously."

"But what about Captain Barton?" asked John. "I mean we don't want to make him wish that he hadn't come to judge."

"Don't worry about him," said Major Holbrooke, "he's only coming because he wants to; he thinks that the Pony Club, or at least this particular branch, is a sort of joke. By the way," he went on, "the test is at eleven sharp and I suggest that each of you practises it through once in the arena between ten and eleven."

"Oh, good," said Noel.

"You're not talking about dressage already?" asked Mrs. Holbrooke, coming in with the post and papers.

"It's all right, we have finished," said the Major. "Have you see anything of Henry yet?" he asked.

"Yes, I heard a violent thumping a few moments ago," said Mrs. Holbrooke.

"He hasn't been punctual for breakfast once this visit," grumbled the Major.

"He's at the tiresome age," said Mrs. Holbrooke soothingly.

"And looks like remaining there," said the Major, picking up *The Times*.

After breakfast there was a discussion about which horse or pony Christopher was to ride. The Major said that he was quite willing to lend the Merry Widow, but that she was a little large for Christopher. Would any larger member care to ride the Widow and loan their pony to Christopher or, alternatively, if everyone wanted to ride their own animal would someone let their pony do the test twice?

Everyone who had a pony offered it at once and Christopher was faced with the embarrassing choice of five ponies. In the end he decided on Wonder. "They're all wizard," he said tactfully, "but I think she's the easiest to ride. Are you sure that you don't mind, Susan?"

"No, not a bit," answered Susan. "Perhaps you'll win the test; I know that I shan't."

"What a hope!" said Christopher.

There followed a frantic hour of sock washing and grooming before the Pony Club members were ready to ride out to the field for their practice.

"Oh, I do feel awful," grumbled Noel.

"Well, stop talking about it, you'll set everyone else off," said Dick.

"Who's going to have first practice?" asked John.

"Bags," said Roger.

"Wonder ought to go fairly early, because she's got to do it twice," said Noel.

"Well, Susan can go second," said Henry. "I'll go third."

"Bags fourth," said John.

"I'm last," said Christopher.

"And I'm last but one," said Noel.

"I suppose I'm last but two, then," said Dick. "It seems to be the only place left."

"I'm collecting steward," said Christopher, producing a megaphone.

"You can't shout loud enough; it ought to be Henry or me," said Roger.

"The Major said I could be, because I haven't a pony to look after and I'm going in last," said Christopher.

"Well, I bags collect you then," said Roger.

Presently the Major appeared and began to offer advice

about riding into the corners and keeping straight on the centre line to the practising competitors and they all learned a lot from watching each other perform.

"Now for the rules," said the Major, when everyone had ridden the test reasonably. "If you take the wrong course, lose your way, we hoot the car horn and you receive two penalty points. No whips or sticks are allowed—unless you are ladies riding side-saddle—and no boots or bandages, that's on the horses, you can wear both. Bridles may be snaffles, pelhams or double bridles; no gags, running reins or martingales. Come on Susan, off with yours—that pony doesn't need it now anyway. The penalty for the use of the voice or the clicking of the tongue is three faults. That's everything, I think; now don't exhaust your horses while we're waiting for Captain Barton." The Major wandered away; Susan took off Wonder's martingale; Blake appeared with a rubber and began to polish the horses' bits and flick invisible specks of dust from their quarters. "Well, you can't all be first," he told the members, but I 'opes that you all do well."

"Here are the judges," shrieked Christopher. "Will the first competitor for the grand dressage test get ready, please."

"It isn't a grand dressage test," shouted Dick. "It's an elementary one."

"Oh, shut up," said Christopher. "I'm collecting steward, not you."

Noel had reached the teeth-chattering stage. John was still trying to memorise the test. "A enter at the ordinary walk," he muttered, "at X, halt and salute."

"The circling's the worst," said Henry. "It's always been my weak point."

"I know I'm not going to do anything in the right place," said Susan. "Wonder says my aids are feeble and doesn't take any notice."

"Well, you needn't worry," said Christopher, "because I'm going to be bottom."

Captain Barton parked his car at C.

"Right, who's coming first?" called the Major, preparing to write down the marks.

"I'm the collecting steward," Christopher reminded him in rather offended accents. "Number one please. Roger Radcliffe on Sky Pilot," he announced.

"Well, here goes," said Roger quite cheerfully as he entered at A, at X he had to halt and salute the judges; he took off his hat with a flourish and grinned broadly.

"They ought to give him five marks for his smile," said Dick.

"I wish I felt like that," said Noel.

"Oh, don't be such a drip, Noel," said Christopher impatiently.

"She's not a drip," said Susan.

"I feel just like one at the moment," said Noel.

They watched critically. Roger's circles at the sitting trot seemed rather pear-shaped and less than the twenty metres in diameter demanded, but his rein-back was good and his circles improved at the canter.

"It doesn't take quite such ages as I thought it would," said Christopher. "Next competitor get ready—who is it? I've forgotten."

"It's me, isn't it?" asked Susan.

"Was that his second change of leg?" asked Dick.

"Yes," answered Noel, "he didn't do too badly this time, but the first one was a bit of a mess. I know that I'm going to forget this loose rein walk at the end," she added.

Everyone clapped furiously as Roger rode out. He was looking quite pleased with himself. "Whew, it's a strain," he said as he dismounted. "I was awful, but at least I didn't go wrong. What did my canter look like?" he asked Hilary.

"Not at all bad," she answered, "the left rein was the best as usual, but why did you trot such tiny circles?"

"Go on, go in," said Christopher to Susan. "Competitor number two," he announced, "Miss Susan Barington-Brown on Golden Wonder."

"Hold hard," shouted the Major. "We haven't finished with number one's marks yet."

Susan waited until they had finished the adding up and then she rode to X, halted and bowed graciously to the judges.

"I don't see why girls shouldn't take their hats off too," complained Christopher.

"Because it would disarrange their hair styles," said Henry.

"Well, June and Merry were the only two of ours with hair styles," said Christopher. "Noel's hair is just a mess, Susan's plaits can't count as a style and Hilary's is straight and such an awful colour that it could look any worse if it *was* disarranged.

"Wonder's going well," said Noel. To everyone's surprise Susan didn't forget any of the test and rode with much more energy than usual. "Jolly good," said the Pony Club members as she rode out, patting Wonder frantically. "Wasn't she marvellous?" said Susan leaping off. "I should think you've won it," said Hilary.

"Don't be silly," answered Susan, "hardly anyone's gone yet and, anyway, Henry's sure to win."

"What nonsense," said Henry vehemently. "I know I've got the best horse, but that isn't everything."

"You haven't got the best horse," said Dick. "You can call her the best schooled, if you like, but the other title is reserved for Crispin."

"He's not a horse," said Christopher.

"Next competitor, *please*," shouted Captain Barton.

"Lawks! Who's next?" asked Christopher.

"Henry Thornton on Black Magic," he announced, as Henry entered the arena. Except for an uncomfortable feeling in the pit of his stomach, Henry was feeling fairly confident. He knew the test and his horse was very well schooled. I ought to be in the first three, he thought, because of Black Magic, but, if I do win, I shan't get half the thrill out of it that the others will if they do, because she's not my horse and I haven't schooled her.

To Noel the chief fault in Henry's performance seemed to lie in his transition from gait to gait; he was inclined to allow Black Magic to become unbalanced. It wasn't a very noticeable fault, in fact none of the other members seemed to see it. Roger only said that Henry was always inaccurate—look at him now backing too many paces. Susan said that Black Magic looked lovely.

"Shockin' performance!" said Henry, grinning as he rode out of the arena.

"No, not at all," said Noel, "one of the best so far."

"John, you're next," said Christopher.

"Don't I know it?" said John ruefully.

"John Manners on Turpin," announced Christopher.

"Dick Turpin," said John indignantly.

"I mean Dick Turpin," announced Christopher.

"Good luck, John," said Noel. John entered the arena with an expression of grim determination, but, inside, he didn't feel at all like that, he felt certain that he was going to make a mess of the whole thing and the two judges, sitting there, waiting to pick his riding to pieces, made him feel even worse.

"Looks a bit glum, don't 'e?" said Christopher as John took off his hat.

"He takes things too seriously," said Dick.

John rode some very creditable circles and Turpin reined-back perfectly and it wasn't until they came to the first change of leg that things went wrong. He cantered past K and then thinking that he had almost finished the test, trotted and prepared to turn up the centre. Suddenly he realised that he was at the wrong end of the arena. He stopped dead and tried to remember what he should be doing, but the whole test seemed to have gone out of his head.

"Change the rein at K," shouted Captain Barton, "with simple change of leg at X."

Thoroughly flustered, John bustled Turpin into a canter on the wrong leg, tore round to F and changed the rein from there. The judges hooted the car horn. John changed the rein again, this time from M. The judges hooted frantically.

"For goodness' sake, stop, boy," shouted Captain Barton.

The Major got out of the car and called, "Wait a minute, John. Just stand still until you've collected your thoughts; there's no hurry."

John stood, scarlet-faced, waiting for his panic to subside.

"Now, start on the right rein, canter at M and change the rein at K, got it?" asked Captain Barton.

"Oh, yes," said John suddenly remembering the whole thing. He turned round and beginning at M finished the test without another mistake. He looked at Turpin's mane when he saluted the judges before leaving the arena and he rode out with a sickly smile which only lasted until he could hide his disappointed face from the other competitors.

"*Bad luck*," said the Pony Club members sympathetically.

"I'm next, Christopher," said Hilary.

"All right, I know, but you can't go yet," said Christopher who didn't like being told his job. "You must wait till the Major gives the signal."

"Well, good luck, Hil," said Roger.

"Miss Hilary Radcliffe on Northwind," announced Christopher. Hilary's performance was very accurate. Every movement was executed on the appropriate spot and every change of gait carried out at the correct marker. Hilary gave the right aids, but they were too obvious; Northwind obeyed them, but without much enthusiasm. The whole affair lacked polish and spirit.

"Richard Hayward on Crispin," announced Christopher.

Dick's performance was a good one. To the other Pony Club members it seemed that, though Crispin hadn't quite as much spirit as Wonder and Black Magic, he was slightly more accurate. His changes of leg were very well timed, but he was not quite as light in hand at the canter as he might have been.

"Are you ready, Noel?" asked Christopher.

"Yes, I hope so," said Noel, looking more miserable than ever.

"Miss Noel Kettering on Sonnet," he announced, as she entered the arena. "Good luck," shouted the Pony Club members, well aware that Noel was in need of moral support. With A glaring at her, she rode up the centre feeling stiff with fear. Why did I ever come on a dressage course? she wondered as she saluted the judges. Here was C, track right. Her nervousness began to leave her; Sonnet's head was just right; a little more impulsion—don't look at the ground. The sequence of the movements flowed through Noel's mind unsought; the time of Sonnet's shortened trot was quite steady, her canter was very slow and yet it lost no impulsion and the little horse seemed as light as air.

"She's jolly good," said Christopher in surprised accents.

"First class," agreed Dick.

"Sonnet's certainly improved," said Hilary rather enviously, and Susan added: "I'm sure Noel's won," in a voice of unaffected pleasure.

"Oy, there's still me to go," objected Christopher. "I'm

going to be the best of all—I don't think. Come on, Roger; I thought you were going to collect me," he added.

"Are the stirrups all right for you, Christopher?" asked Susan.

Noel rode out of the arena and jumped off. "You *were* good," she told Sonnet, "much better than I expected."

"I should imagine you'll be among the first three," said Henry, leading Black Magic across to Noel.

"Do watch," said Susan to Noel. "I want to know if Wonder went as well as this for me."

"She had a bit more impulsion when you rode her," said Noel.

"He's doing awfully well," said Susan, "I mean when you think that he's only had one short practice." Christopher was perfectly happy. He had decided that he hadn't the ghost of a chance of being in the first three and therefore he might as well take things easily. Wonder was grand, he thought. In some ways she was a relief after Fireworks, but he wouldn't want her as his own pony he decided—she wasn't dashing enough. Oh, he had forgotten what he was supposed to do next. At E circle left, he had done that. "Oy, I'm stuck," he shouted to the judges. "Canter at M," shouted Captain Barton.

"Thanks a lot," said Christopher. He finished the test successfully and as he rode out, grinning gaily, he said to the other members, "Wasn't I a fool? I was thinking of something else."

"Now for the results," said Roger.

"I'm out of it anyway," said John gloomily.

"I'm hungry," said Christopher.

"Ugh," said Noel. "I couldn't eat a thing." Captain Barton got out of his car. "Come over here, please," he shouted. The Pony Club members hurried in his direction, except for John, who followed more slowly.

"I can see that you're in a hurry to hear the results,"

said Captain Barton, "and so I will refrain from making a speech and merely announce, with great pleasure, that first was Miss Noel Kettering on Sonnet."

"Second, Henry Thornton on Black Magic, third Richard Hayward and fourth Miss Susan Barington-Brown. None of the other people were very far behind and I'm glad to say that no one gave a bad performance, in fact, if you all do as well at the hunter trials on Saturday I feel sure that Major Holbrooke will win his ten pounds—and a very well deserved ten pounds it is too."

"Hear, hear," said Dick.

"Would the winners come up for their rosettes, please?" said Major Holbrooke.

"Gosh!" said Noel, scrambling on Sonnet.

"Golly," said Susan, "I never expected rosettes."

"Big of Uncle George," said Henry, mounting too. The winners rode up to the judges and Captain Barton said, "There's a prize for the winner and a very suitable one too," and he handed Noel a red rosette and a pair of blunt spurs.

"Oh, thanks awfully," said Noel, "but surely I'm not good enough to wear them?"

"You'd better ask the Major about that," said Captain Barton as he handed the rosettes to the other winners. The unlucky Pony Club members clapped loudly and the Major said, "It is now time for lunch."

CHAPTER ELEVEN

ON Friday morning Fireworks was sound and the Major suggested that, as the horse boxes were not coming until after an early lunch, the Pony Club members might like to practise for the pair class for a short time in the paddock. Everyone thought this an excellent idea and Henry and Roger arranged a few low, wide jumps. Turpin and Crispin once again made a perfect pair and Christopher pulled up his girths every five minutes and Noel grumbled about the needle until Dick told her that she was anti-social and Hilary said, "For goodness' sake, shut up."

After they had cleaned their tack and given the horses a brush over so that they would look tidy for Colonel Shellbourne, the Pony Club members settled down on the grass plot in the middle of the yard, intending to enjoy the sunshine for half an hour before lunch. Just as everyone was comfortably relaxed, the Major appeared with a long list of things which, he said, must on no account be forgotten as he didn't want a wailing and a gnashing of teeth at ten o'clock on Saturday morning. He asked, "Is everyone packed? Have you all the clothes you need for Saturday, something to wear at dinner to-night, washing things and pyjamas?"

"Won't a nightie do?" inquired Christopher in tones of assumed horror.

"Well, I want all the luggage out here on the grass," said the Major, ignoring Christopher, "arranged neatly with your saddles, bridles, grooming tools, needles and thread for plaiting, riding sticks and hard hats."

Henry groaned. "We might as well be in the army," he muttered, using Christopher to pull himself to his feet. "The horses will travel in head collars, and leg and tail bandages," said the Major.

The people who came daily to Folly Court had their suitcases in the saddle room, but the others had to walk to the house, which they considered a tremendous hardship. They climbed the stairs grumbling that they were steep and that the weather was hot and pulling themselves up by the bannisters. It was lunch time when everything was arranged to the Major's satisfaction and after lunch, just as everyone was beginning to look out for the horse boxes, Noel's nose began to bleed. Blake said, "It's the hot weather, sir; we'll 'ave a storm before night." Fortunately the horse boxes were a little late and by the time that the horses had been boxed and Christopher had fetched his toothbrush, which he had forgotten to pack, Noel's nose had stopped bleeding. At last everyone, feeling hot and rather bad-tempered, was packed in the two horse boxes. Sky Pilot, Golden Wonder and Black Magic were in the proper horse box and the other ponies in the cattle truck They reached Dalstone Manor, Colonel Shellbourne's house, in time for tea. Everyone came to life as the horse boxes turned up the drive.

"Hurray," said John peering out of the truck. Noel pushed her hair out of her eyes and said, "Thank goodness." "Your face is dirty," Hilary told her. "Where?" asked Noel, scrubbing hastily with a handkerchief. Dalstone Manor was a medium-sized cream-coloured house with green doors and windows. The paint was new; the garden had weedless paths, orderly flower beds and a newly mown lawn. The horse boxes pulled up outside the stables—a straight line of solid, well-built, brick buildings with the grooms' quarters above. Colonel Shellbourne's four stout hunters, just up from grass, looked out and whinnied. Colonel Shellbourne greeted the Major while the Pony Club members unloaded the horses' tack and luggage. "Well, now," he said as the Major gave the drivers their instructions for the return journey, "we'd better stow these animals away; I expect all you youngsters are ready for your teas."

"I feel as though I ought to give a little buck," said Henry quietly. "Youngsters indeed!"

"Shush," said Noel. Susan giggled. Colonel Shellbourne told the Major that he had two paddocks beside the house for the horses and the Major said that the three mares were to have the smaller paddock and the geldings the other. "The mares all know each other," he said, "but I don't suppose the geldings will kick if there's no disturbing influence." When the horses were settled, the Colonel led the members, each carrying a suitcase and a hard hat, into the house. The inside of the house was not nearly so immaculate as the outside led one to expect. Everything was a little faded and the sofas looked as though the dogs were allowed to sit on them, as indeed they were.

"I'm afraid that the arrangements are a bit primitive," said Colonel Shellbourne, "but you must forgive us; we've never had nine people to stay before. Ah, here we are, Hazel," he said to his wife, a slightly stooping, grey-haired woman of about sixty, with a long aquiline nose and alert grey eyes. The Major introduced each of them in turn and they all dropped their possessions as they tried to shake hands. They were told to leave their luggage in the hall, which was hung with sporting prints, masks, pads, brushes and hunting horns, and, having washed, to assemble for tea in the dining-room. After tea the horses were each given a large feed—the Major had brought a stack of oats—and then the members were shown to their rooms. Susan and Noel were sharing a guest room. Hilary had a small bedroom to herself. John and Henry shared another room and Roger, Dick and Christopher had a children's room with bunks and a camp bed, which Roger and Dick at once said would do for Christopher.

Then everyone wanted baths and there were only two bathrooms, one of which had been taken possession of by the Major, while the Pony Club members had been inspecting each other's rooms. After a lot of arguing and bagging the matter was organised and no one was allowed more than eight minutes. During dinner the long-expected storm broke; the thunder and lightning were distant, but the rain teemed down and lay in pools on the dry ground. Henry said that the going would be heavy and Susan, who was slightly afraid of thunder, said that she hoped Wonder wouldn't be frightened or stand under a tree and be struck. Noel was talking to Colonel Shellbourne about Sonnet and telling him what a nice pony she was; for it was he who had given her to Noel. The Major was talking to Mrs. Shellbourne—who wasn't a very horsy character—about a play, which neither of them had seen.

By the time the Pony Club members were sent to bed—which, to their indignation, was very early—the storm was over. The horses were grazing peacefully in the paddocks, an occasional bird twittered in the garden, the air felt fresh and cool.

"I'm awfully excited about to-morrow," said Susan, who was lying in bed, to Noel, standing at the window.

"So am I," agreed Noel, half drawing the faded chintz curtains and crossing the room to her bed, "except that it means the end of the course."

"That's true," said Susan.

"I *have* enjoyed it so," said Noel sadly. "I never expected it to be such fun."

"Well, we must persuade the Major to have another next summer," said Susan brightly, "he might have a show jumping course."

"What a hope," said Noel drearily, "he's probably fed up and just longing for Sunday to come."

"Well, we've still got to-morrow," said Susan, "and you always were one to look on the dark side."

At half-past six, when the Pony Club members—with a good deal of whispering—stole downstairs and out into the garden, the day was cool and low grey clouds filled the sky.

"I hope it's not going to rain," said John loudly as he put on his shoes on the front door step.

"Shush, you idiot," said Henry just as loudly, "do you want to wake the whole house?"

"For goodness' sake come on," shouted Hilary from the garden gate. "I can't think why boys take so long to put on their shoes."

"They don't," shouted Christopher in reply, "we started dressing after you."

"For heaven's sake shut up," said Henry, "don't you realise that you're bang under Uncle G.'s window?"

"Lawks," said Christopher in horror.

By the time that all the horses were caught, put in loose-boxes or tied to rings in the stable walls and fed, it was seven o'clock and Colonel Shellbourne's tall, gloomy groom, appropriately named Gaunt, appeared and fed his horses. He told Noel where to get the hot water for washing Sonnet, who had managed to cover herself in mud and grass stains as well as the normal grime. When Gaunt had had breakfast, he appeared again and gave Noel some blue bag to go in Sonnet's rinsing water; he also told Christopher not to let Fireworks eat the Colonel's best cherry tree. At eight o'clock Major Holbrooke came out to tell the Pony Club members that it was nearly time for breakfast; he found Noel almost in hysterics because she had used too much blue bag and Sonnet was now pale blue all over. He said that he thought she looked rather elegant and after all fashionable women went about with blue hair, so why not Sonnet? But Gaunt was more helpful; he told Noel to rinse her again with plain water and that she wouldn't look nearly so blue when she was dry. After a quick breakfast everyone whose animal had a mane, began to plait. Henry, who had never plaited a mane before, surprised everyone by putting up Black Magic's quite reasonably, far better than Wonder's long, loose loops, or Fireworks' wispy lumps.

John, who had no mane to plait or socks to wash, obligingly gave all the tack a final polish. At half-past nine everyone was ready to start and shortly afterwards they were on their way, led by Gaunt, on the Colonel's Nimrod, along the winding road, through a countryside of smaller fields and larger trees than they knew at home. Colonel and Mrs. Shellbourne and the Major passed them in the car; they were going on ahead to make the entries and collect the numbers. The Major joined the members as they entered the showground. "Here are your numbers," he said handing them round. "It's a very nice little course. You're in the Ist Class, Christopher—don't forget to tighten your girths. John, Susan, Noel, Hilary and Dick are in Class II, Henry and Roger in Class III and Class IV is the pairs."

"You'd better walk the course," said Colonel Shellbourne, "get the lie of the land, you know. The Major, Gaunt and I can hold the horses." The Pony Club members walked round. Noel and Susan exclaimed with horror at the size of each jump; the Radcliffes contradicted them scornfully. Henry grumbled that everything would be higher for him—though only two of the fences were adjustable. Christopher groaned because there was a gate to open and he was sure that Fireworks was going to jump it.

"Well?" asked the Major when they returned to the

collecting ring. "It's awful," said Susan, "there's a horrid drop after the second hedge."

"Oh *Susan,*" said Hilary, "it's tiny."

"This isn't as stiff as the practice course," said Dick.

"And I like the sheep-pen," said Roger, "it looks easy."

"Yes, so long as you keep your horse straight," said the Major, "the jump over which you're most likely to fault," he went on, "is the post and rails out in the middle of the field. If you don't get your horses together for that, they'll either stop or go straight through it. Have you tightened your girths?" he asked Christopher, as the collecting steward called Class I into the collecting ring; he sent the first competitor to the start and the hunter trials had begun.

"Christopher is sixth," said Colonel Shellbourne, who seemed to be enjoying himself. "Good luck, my boy, good luck."

There were a great many entries, because several pony clubs, besides the organising branch, were taking part, and to save time the starter was starting a second competitor when the first was half-way round the course; this made Christopher's turn come quite quickly. He watched the first competitor, a tall, dark girl with plaits on a thickset pony without a noseband, refuse three times at the first fence—a made-up brush. The next three competitors completed the course, but one of them knocked down the rails, another bungled the gate and the third was very slow. The girl, who was started immediately before Christopher, was riding a flashy-looking chestnut in a jointed pelham and a running martingale; he looked as though he could gallop but she seemed afraid to let him go, but at each fence she tugged and jerked at his mouth in an attempt to bring him back to hand. When she was half-way round the course, the starter dropped the flag and away went Fireworks, obviously in pursuit of the chestnut. "Steady old man," cried Christopher as he galloped towards the first fence, but

Fireworks still had a little speed in reserve, he lengthened his stride and cleared the fence easily. The next field was downhill and at the bottom was a sharp turn and the hedge with the drop into a stubble field with rails and the sheep-pen in the middle of it. Christopher, who had been riding well forward with his weight in his stirrups, remembered to sit down to collect Fireworks for the rails and to steady him again for the sheep-pen. He cleared them both; then there was another hedge, this time with a ditch on the take off, ahead was the gate. "Whoa, Fireworks, whoa," said Christopher pulling on the reins. He could feel that the pony wanted to jump it, but he managed to turn him sideways and stop beside it. It was an easy gate to open and shut and they were through in a moment and galloping on. Fireworks was galloping even faster and suddenly Christopher noticed the girl on the chestnut jumping a brush fence which stood in the middle of the field in which he was galloping. "Oh lawks," he said aloud. "Well, I suppose I'm meant to overtake her." He rode at the brush fence, cleared it and galloped on, decreasing the distance which separated him from the chestnut at every stride. Ahead was a sharp turn through a half-open gate beside a straw stack; he would wait till he was through there and then pass her before the next fence. "Come on," he said to Fireworks. He caught up with the girl; for a moment they were side by side; he heard the drumming of her pony's hoofs and saw her set face and then Fireworks drew ahead. They were galloping uphill now, the next jump was a stout post and rails in a hedge and then the last fence, a hedge with a ditch and past the white flag that marked the finish. Christopher jumped off Fireworks and led him back to the collecting ring, patting him and feeding him on handfuls of oats.

"Well done," said Major Holbrooke.

"A magnificent round; congratulations, my boy, congratulations," roared Colonel Shellbourne excitedly.

"Jolly good, Christopher," said the other Pony Club members.

"He's won it," said the Colonel firmly, "obviously a clear win."

"There are a good many more to go yet," the Major reminded him. "Maybe, maybe," said Colonel Shellbourne, "but they can't go any faster." Colonel Shellbourne was right. Two other competitors made clear rounds, but their times were nothing like as good as Christopher's and, when the numbers of the winners were called out, his was first. "Hurray," said the Pony Club members.

"Well done, well done," said Colonel Shellbourne. Christopher rode to the judges' wagon for his rosette.

"We've started well," said Hilary.

"Yes, I feel it's a good omen," said Henry.

"Look at that," said John, as Christopher rode back clasping a large cup.

"Oh, Christopher," said Susan.

"Class II in the collecting ring, please," announced the steward. "Number 14 at the start. Number 14," he called again, and "come along, number 14," when no one rode forward. "Noel, you're number 14, shrieked Susan suddenly.

"Go on, Noel," said Henry.

"There's no need to get flustered," said the Major hastily, as Noel shot forward at a canter. "Keep calm, there's plenty of time."

"Number fifteen get ready," said the collecting steward. The starter dropped his flag and Noel was off. Sonnet cleared the first hedge and galloped down the hill; she hesitated a little at the hedge with the drop, but Noel used her legs and she went over. The rails were higher now, but Sonnet cleared them and the sheep-pen; she stood well at the gate and then, not seeming at all tired, galloped on.

She took off too early for the brush in the middle of the field, but managed to clear it. Noel steadied her for the half-open gate; she was on the right leg. But they took the corner a little too easily and coming into the next field at the wrong angle, Noel missed the flagged fence and jumped lower down the hedge. As soon as she was over she realised what she had done. She looked back; yes, she was off the course. "Oh, Sonnet, I'm sorry," she said and, jumping the last fence, rode miserably into the collecting ring.

"You're disqualified," said Roger.

"You were an idiot," said Hilary, "didn't you see the flags?"

"You'd have had a pretty good chance otherwise," said Christopher.

"Dick's hit the rails," said the Major, creating a diversion, which was lucky, for Noel felt near to tears. It was so awful to have let Sonnet down when she had cleared every fence. She patted her and gave her a handful of oats. "I don't think the omen is much use," said Roger. "Good luck," he shouted to Hilary as she started. "Bad luck," they said to Dick as he rode in.

"How's Hilary doing?" asked Dick.

"Quite well, so far," replied Roger, "but she's a bit slow." John's number was called and he rode down to the start. Turpin was feeling fresh, but he stood quite quietly as he waited for the flag. Hilary had cleared the sheep-pen when John was started. He rammed his hat on, saw the pricked roan ears in front of him and rode at the middle of the first fence. Turpin cleared it easily. Fast down the hill, but one would have to steady for the turn at the bottom, thought John. Now those beastly rails. "Steady, Turpin, steady."

"Good jump," said the Major in the collecting ring.

"First class, first class," agreed his cousin Harry.

"Come on Turpin," said John when they landed over the sheep-pen. "We've got to gallop." Turpin was very helpful over the gate; he pushed it with his nose when John had unlatched it and helped to shut it with his chest. Hilary wasn't very far ahead now, John leaned forward and galloped in pursuit. They gained on her still more and finished with only one small field between them. "Those were two fearfully good rounds," said Christopher, "and Susan's doing well too. She's going much faster than she did at home." Susan arrived flushed and breathless. "Wonder was marvellous," she gasped, "she went awfully fast and yet she stopped perfectly at the gate. Didn't she jump the rails beautifully?"

"She made a very good round," said the Major. "All three of you did, but I think that John's was the fastest time."

"That's all our lot for this class then," said Christopher. "Who's this going round now? It looks as though it was afraid to go out of a collected canter, what a drip!"

A tall girl on a stout, long-tailed bay cob followed the boy who wouldn't let his pony gallop; she made a good round, until she came to the half-open gate; there she took the corner on the wrong leg and the cob fell sideways. His rider wasn't hurt and she remounted quickly and jumped the last two fences, but of course she was out of the running. A boy on a blood pony galloped round at a tremendous pace, but brushed through every fence, and another boy on a grey, dock-tailed cob cleared all the fences, but seemed rather slow. A very smart pony refused the first fence three times and an untidy one, with dirty tack and an unpulled mane and tail, made a very good round indeed and cast all the West Barsetshire members into the depths of despair. A very small girl on a tall and rather thin pony trotted solemnly round the course and a girl, who shouted at her skewbald, instead of using her legs, had three refusals at the sheep-pen, and then the collecting steward announced that that was all the entries for Class II and would competitors for Class III come into the collecting ring. There was a long and nerve-racking wait while the judges added up the marks. John felt quite certain that, in spite of what the Major had said, he had been slower than Susan, Hilary and the untidy pony. But still, a reserve rosette would be enough to restore his self-respect which had been shattered by the dressage competition. Susan thought, I *should* love Wonder to win another rosette, but it's a lot to expect after Thursday, and Hilary thought, well, I did a clear round but so did John and Susan, the untidy pony and the grey cob—all five of us can't have rosettes. At last the judges came to their decision: First John, second the untidy pony, third Susan and reserve Hilary.

"Hurray, hurray," said Christopher, throwing his crash cap into the air and failing to catch it.

"This is frightful," said Henry to Roger. "We shall have to make an effort to acquire a cup after the example set us by our youngsters. Look at John's 'trophy'; it's even larger and uglier than Christopher's."

"They're both *super* cups," said Christopher indignantly.

"Are you number 31?" the collecting steward asked Roger and when he replied that he was, "Right, you're next and you," he said to Henry, "follow him."

Roger rode down to the start. The rails were much higher now, he thought, looking round the course. He pulled up his stirrups a hole and fidgeted with his reins. Most of the horses looked faster than Pilot, he thought, but still he was a good jumper.

"Are you ready?" asked the starter. He dropped his flag and Roger was on his way.

Roger and Henry both made clear rounds. Henry was the faster until he came to the gate, where Black Magic wasted several precious seconds by refusing to stand for him to shut it. Later in the competition there was another very good round made by a girl on a grey blood horse and she wasted no time at the gate. By the end of the class the judges were evidently thinking about lunch for the collecting stewards brutally announced that the results of Class III would be given *after* the interval.

"Dirty devils," said Christopher loudly.

"Oh, well, I know I haven't won anything," said Henry, "so they won't keep me in suspense *or* spoil my appetite."

"We'd better tie these animals up somewhere," said the Major. "John, would you fetch the head-collars from the car?"

Colonel Shellbourne found dozens of places to tie the ponies, but the Major said that they were all dangerous for some reason or other. However, by the time they had all been allowed a short drink, he had found some suitable railings, to which they could all be tied without being in kicking distance of each other. When the owners had each given their mounts a small feed, they joined the grown-ups at the Shellbourne's car for lunch, which was substantial with two hard-boiled eggs each, a mountain of sandwiches and cake and a basket of apples.

The sun came out for a few brief moments when the Pony Club members were bridling their ponies for the last class, but it disappeared again as they were called into the collecting ring. They rode round in pairs, practising and arguing about which would let the other down. The first pair was hopeless. It consisted of two sisters wearing crash caps over a mass of frizzled hair and mounted on fat, dappled grey ponies. One jumped the first fence but the other refused. She rode at it again with waving legs. "Hit him, hit him," shrieked her sister and the refuser obediently flapped her stick on the pony's shoulder, without putting her reins in one hand; the sister shrieked, "Hit him," even louder, but it was all in vain, he refused once more and the judge blew his hunting horn. "You should have hit him harder," said one sister to the other as they rode back through the collecting ring. The next pair completed the course, but they were rather slow and one of them knocked down the rails. They were followed by the boy who had ridden at a collected canter and the girl on the cob which had fallen. They were very fast but couldn't keep together, for the blood pony was out of control and the cob, though galloping his fastest, could not keep up. The girl on the grey horse, which had made such a good round in the associate class, had a hopeless partner, who fell off at the sheep-pen, and the next three pairs all made mistakes of some sort. Then there was a pair which kept together and cleared all the fences but never galloped until the finish, and another pair, which was very good except that one partner got left behind at the sheep-pen for a few moments. Turpin and Crispin looked a very well-matched pair as they rode to the start. The two ponies were the same size and almost the same build—Turpin being a little heavier than Crispin—and the two boys were both wearing breeches and brown tweed coats. They started quietly, but gradually increased their speed, until they were galloping; they made a very good jump over the in and out, both ponies taking off and landing together. John opened the gate, Dick said, "Thank you," as he rode through. They galloped on barely speaking a word save for Dick's "O.K." as he sent Crispin on for each fence; they finished in the same effortless style and rode back to the collecting ring.

"Well done," said the Major, "that was an excellent performance." Colonel Shellbourne, speechless with delight, could only splutter incoherently and pat the boys on the back. Susan and Hilary were already half-way round the course, but they were not keeping together very well and the Major said that Northwind had knocked down the rails. When they were nearing the finish, Roger and Henry were started. They began well and made quite a good pair, though Black Magic always forged ahead at the fences, because she jumped faster than Sky Pilot, until they came to the half-open gate. Then Roger, on the inside, was going too fast; he took the corner too wide and left no room for Henry, who pulled up sharply with an agonised shriek of "Steady, you idiot; let me catch up." After that Henry was disheartened and his riding went to pieces as he finished the course. Noel and Christopher were on their way and they were the noisiest pair of all. At each fence Christopher shouted, "Come on, I can't go any slower. Catch up quickly," he shrieked if Sonnet was the smallest bit behind, so Noel raced to keep level all the way to the gate, which she opened. "Oh do be quick," shouted Christopher impatiently as she shut it. "Come on," he said as they rode at the brush. Fireworks refused to slow down much for the half-open gate, but, as he was on the outside, they got through with considerably less difficulty than Roger and Henry. "Come on, gallop," shouted Christopher as they crossed the last field. "That was wonderful," said Noel as she pulled up after passing the winning post. "Wizard," agreed Christopher.

"I was terrified that your saddle was going to slip or that I was going to be left miles behind," Noel went on.

"Well neither happened," said Christopher, "and I don't think that we were too bad really—considering who it was."

"Good effort," said Henry as they joined the party in the collecting ring; "you were much better than us."

"Not at all bad," agreed the Major.

"Not bad! By Jove, that's faint praise," objected Colonel Shellbourne. "Yes indeed, I should say first——" but he was drowned by the collecting steward, who announced,

"Here are the results of Class III. First, Miss Claire Dinyard; second," and the West Barsetshire members held their breath, "Mr. Roger Radcliffe, third Mr. Henry Thornton, reserve Miss Annette March." The West Barsetshire people were delighted, they skipped about saying, "Jolly good," and clapped loudly when the winners were given their rosettes. "In a moment I shall be able to give you the results of Class IV," said the collecting steward. Henry and Roger tied their horses' rosettes on their bridles and told them how clever they were. "Thank you for letting me ride her, Uncle George," said Henry.

"Not at all; it's been a pleasure," answered the Major, "and this little course is just what she needed to give her confidence."

"Oh, dear," said Noel, "the hunter trials are over."

"All good things come to an end," said Susan brightly.

"Here are the results of Class IV," said the collecting steward. "First, John Manners and Richard Hayward; second, Alice and Stephen Kale; third, Noel Kettering and Christopher Minton; reserve Celia and Catherine Maleworth-Jones." Everyone clapped as the winners rode up to the wagon, Colonel Shellbourne the loudest of all.

"This is terrific," said Christopher to Noel. "Yes, I never expected anything," she replied, patting Sonnet.

"Well, you haven't done too badly," said the Major, smiling slightly. "Give that cup to the colonel, Dick; he's got a jeweller's shop in the car. Has anyone seen a head collar? I've only got seven. Somebody collect the tail bandages."

"Congratulations, all of you," said Colonel Shellbourne. "By Jove, yes. Never seen anything like it, never. Swept the board, by Jove. Well, well, I've lost my bet, but I've never been more happy to lose one, I can promise you that. I suppose you did teach them dressage, George?"

"Yes, there's no doubt about that," answered the Major; "we'll stage a test for you if you like."

"No, no, not in my line of country at all," said the Colonel hastily. "I'll take you at your word."

"Well, home to tea," said Mrs. Shellbourne, getting into the car already laden with head collars, tail bandages, cups and dogs.

"There's no need to hurry back to the Manor," the Major told the Pony Club members. "The horse boxes won't be there until five-thirty, so there's plenty of time for feeds and tea."

"O.K.," they answered cheerfully and Christopher added, "we must sing all the way."

"Thank heaven I'm not coming with you then," said the Major rudely and the car drove away. The Pony Club members mounted and saying good night to the collecting steward and one or two other people, who had spoken to them, they rode homewards.

"What a day," said Roger.

"It *was* pretty good, wasn't it?" said John.

"Absolutely super," shouted Christopher from the back of the cavalcade.

"I was an idiot," said Noel.

"Ssh, no recriminations," said Henry. "We've had a good time, the horses have jumped marvellously and we've won Uncle G. his wager; nothing else matters."

"I should say that your Uncle G. has won his own wager," said Dick, "after all, he's improved us."

"True," said Henry. "We ought to present him with a silver cigarette case suitably inscribed, but, as he already has six, it wouldn't be much use."

"We must give him three hearty cheers, before we go home to-night," said Roger.

Henry shuddered, "No, for pity's sake," he said.

"Why not?" asked John.

"I think the Major would rather we all thanked him separately," said Noel.

"We shall have to write thank you letters too," said Susan.

"Oh, I do wish everything wasn't over," complained Noel.

"Same here," said John. "We've had a jolly good time, much better than I expected."

"Evelyn said that dressage would be dreary," said Roger. "I think she was wrong, don't you, Hil?"

"Yes, but I suppose people like different things," said Hilary.

"Still, if they're horsy they ought to want to ride well, whatever they like," said Dick, "and that's where dressage comes in."

The grey sky with its suspicious look of rain was growing darker and the air seemed filled with the first thoughts of autumn. A calm melancholy lay over the land and found its way into the hearts of the Pony Club members. The summer was over; the brave, golden days were done, but they had memories to last until the next one.

"Oh, do let's sing," said Christopher. "We're half-way home already."

"Keep right on to the end of the road," sang the Pony Club members loudly, but not very tunefully.

'JINNY AT FINMORY' BOOKS

by Patricia Leitch

Armada Originals

FOR LOVE OF A HORSE

Red-haired Jinny Manders has always dreamt of owning a horse. When she rescues Shantih, a chestnut Arab mare, from a cruel circus, her wish seems about to come true. But Shantih escapes on to the moors above their home where Jinny despairs of ever getting near her again.

A DEVIL TO RIDE

Shantih, safe for the first time in her life, in the Manders' stable, is inseparable from her new mistress. But she is impossible to ride, and Jinny can't control her . . .

THE SUMMER RIDERS

Jinny is furious when Marlene, the brash city girl, comes to stay and insists on riding Shantih. But when Marlene's brother, Bill, gets into trouble with the local police, Jinny and Shantih are the only ones who can stop him being prosecuted.

NIGHT OF THE RED HORSE

When archaeologists come to Finmory to excavate an ancient site, Jinny and Shantih mysteriously and terrifyingly fall under the power of ancient Celtic 'Pony Folk'.

GALLOP TO THE HILLS

Jinny's special friend, Ken, leaves Finmory and his dog, Kelly, disappears. Sheep are killed on the moor and local farmers set out to hunt Kelly down – and Jinny and Shantih find themselves involved in a desperate race to save him.

HORSE IN A MILLION

Life seems to fall apart for Jinny when Shantih disappears from her field one night. Desperate to find her, Jinny begins a desperate race against time – a race that takes her away from the wild Finmory hills and into danger.